W9-CIC-374

MAGIC ZERO

BOOK FOUR

BATTLE FOR ARCANUM

Also by Thomas E. Sniegoski
and Christopher Golden

Magic Zero

Dragon Secrets

Ghostfire

MAGIC ZERO
BOOK FOUR

BATTLE FOR ARCANUM

Previously published as *Wurm War*

Thomas E. Sniegoski

and

Christopher Golden

Aladdin

New York   London   Toronto   Sydney   New Delhi

ALADDIN

An imprint of Simon & Schuster Children's Publishing Division

1230 Avenue of the Americas, New York, NY 10020

First Aladdin hardcover edition August 2013

Copyright © 2005 by Christopher Golden and Thomas E. Sniegoski

Originally published as Outcast: *Wurm War*

All rights reserved, including the right of reproduction in whole or in part in any form.

ALADDIN is a trademark of Simon & Schuster, Inc.,

and related logo is a registered trademark of Simon & Schuster, Inc.

Also available in an Aladdin paperback edition.

For information about special discounts for bulk purchases, please contact Simon & Schuster Special Sales at 1-866-506-1949 or business@simonandschuster.com.

The Simon & Schuster Speakers Bureau can bring authors to your live event.

For more information or to book an event contact the Simon & Schuster Speakers Bureau at 1-866-248-3049 or visit our website at www.simonspeakers.com.

The text of this book was set in Bembo Std.

Manufactured in the United States of America 0713 FFG

2 4 6 8 10 9 7 5 3 1

Library of Congress Control Number 2004109150

ISBN 978-1-4424-7316-4 (hc)

ISBN 978-1-4424-7315-7 (pbk)

ISBN 978-1-4391-1342-4 (eBook)

For June Rae Jewell and family, with love

Thanks and love to Connie and the kids, Nicholas, Daniel, and Lily Grace. Much thanks to Tom, of course, and to editor extraordinaire Samantha Schutz. Thanks are also due to the unusual suspects: Jose Nieto and Lisa Delissio, Rick Hautala, Amber Benson, Bob Tomko, Lisa Clancy, Ashleigh Bergh, and Allie Costa. And finally, thanks to Pete Donaldson, Jay Sanders, Charlie Mitchell, Adam Rosen, and Jason Lust, for all their hard work and enthusiasm.

—C. G.

For Samantha ("Bugsy") Stanley. Didn't want you to feel left out.

Special thanks to LeeAnne for going beyond the call of duty, and to Mulder for allowing me to be his faithful manservant. Thanks to Mom and Dad Sniegoski, Dave Kraus, Liesa Abrams, Harry and Hugo, David Carroll, Ken Curtis, Jon and Flo, Bob and Pat, Lisa Clancy, Abbie and Kim, and the inmates over at Cole's Comics.

And an extra-special thank-you to Samantha Schutz for all her hard work on this series. Thanks, Sam.

—T. S.

PROLOGUE

SkyHaven was falling, and it was all Timothy's fault.

The world of Terra ran entirely on magic. It was within everything and everyone, with a single exception—Timothy Cade, the only person on Terra who had no capacity for magic. Behind his back, the mages snickered and called him the un-magician. It was a slur, an insult, but it was true.

Magic had no affect on him, and if he so much as touched anything enchanted, he would temporarily unravel spells that even the most powerful Wizards of Old could not have broken. Not only that, but recently he discovered that if he concentrated hard enough, he could stretch the nullifying field that surrounded him, so he didn't even have to touch magic to disrupt it.

Timothy had always thought of the effect he had on magic—and his inability to perform even the simplest spell—as an affliction. But more and more he had been finding that it was what made him unique, and that there was strength in him that he had never known. Magic itself was pure, but if the intentions of the mage wielding it were cruel or evil, the magic became dark and deadly.

Never had there been a wizard as dark and cruel as Alhazred. Long thought to be dead, he had returned with an insidious plan. He had been kidnapping and killing mages so that he could absorb their magic. Worse, he had collected thousands of ghostfire lamps—lights powered by the magical spirit essence of dead mages—and was consuming the magic from their lingering souls. But that was only the beginning. Alhazred had begun to tap into the magical matrix—the very source of all the magic in the world—and once he took control of that, no one would be able to stand against him.

Timothy knew he had to do something.

Focusing on the tingling sensation of the magic as it slid over him, he pushed and felt the null field ballooning around him—expanding. It took every ounce of will and inner strength he could muster to force the field away from himself, spreading and stretching to encompass the entire massive chamber, and beyond.

Alhazred's eyes had darkened in anger as every ghostfire lamp, every piece of spell-glass in the room, shattered in a single moment, releasing the energies of the dead mages in a blinding flash. For the briefest of moments, Timothy felt triumphant.

And then SkyHaven—an island fortress that floated above the ocean—began to fall from the sky.

His mind cried out in panic. Through fear and instinct, he drew the null field back to himself, and the freefall of SkyHaven came to an abrupt and stomach-flipping stop.

The realization of what he had done gradually sank in.

I've disrupted the whole matrix, he thought. *Everything must have winked out for a second, all of the magical power in the area . . . and maybe farther. . . .*

Suddenly he was very afraid, distracted only by the dark wizard's pitiful howl of defeat. Timothy watched as Alhazred at last began to die, his gray flesh withering and crinkling like burning parchment. Darkness puffed out of him, and soon there was nothing left of the evil archmage but drifting ash on the floor.

And with Alhazred at last defeated, Timothy's thoughts painfully returned to what he had done, how he had reached out and touched the power of the world.

"Are you okay?" Cassandra Nicodemus asked from somewhere in the darkness of the chamber.

Timothy could not even begin to answer that question.

CHAPTER ONE

The intensity of the buzzing hum inside his thick, horned skull nearly forced Verlis from the sky above Tora'nah. He faltered and began to drop, but quickly regained his senses, flapping his leathery wings all the harder, and soaring upward again. His heart hammered in his broad chest, and alarms of danger raced through him. The last time he had experienced this hum, he had been wearing a helmet forged of Malleum—the metal tied intrinsically to his kind, the descendants of dragons known as the Wurm.

But now it appeared that he didn't need the helmet to feel this connection.

Verlis sped through the air toward the magical barrier between dimensions that separated Terra from Draconae, the world to which the Wurm had been banished many decades past. It was called Alhazred's Divide. On the other side was a Wurm civilization of savagery and tyranny, lorded over by a general called Raptus, who wanted nothing more than for his sorcerers to tear down the Veil so that he and his army could invade Terra and destroy the world of mages.

Filled with a terrible dread, Verlis spread his wings and hovered before the barrier. The light of Alhazred's Divide shone from ground to sky, from horizon to horizon, as it had for centuries, but now its ethereal light had dimmed. The hum in Verlis's skull increased and he hissed in pain, flinching away from the magical barrier.

As it winked out, all the magic in Tora'nah cut off for just a moment.

A moment was long enough. The barrier fell with a sound like breaking glass, the spell at last destroyed, and with a murderous roar of triumph, the barbaric Wurm that had been trying to break it down from the other side began to come through. The sky beyond—the sky of Draconae—was filled with dark, winged figures, the Wurm gathering like storm clouds as they realized what had happened.

The first wave emerged on foot, cautiously, from the large rip that had been torn in the fabric of reality. The edges of the dimensional tear hissed and sputtered. Verlis watched them come, for a moment unable to believe that the barrier had been broken, and then he remembered the mages at the mining operation nearby, digging for the precious metal Malleum, and realized their safety was now in jeopardy.

Spurred to action, Verlis swooped down out of the sky

toward the invaders. He opened his massive jaws and a stream of liquid fire erupted from his gullet, bathing them in flames as he flew past and away. They were his kinsmen, these Wurm, but not like him at all. They had waged a civil war upon his clan, who wanted only peace. To him they were the enemy.

Two of the Wurm soldiers roared in pain as Verlis's fire engulfed them, and the others were distracted by his attack, some even hesitating on the threshold of this world. But Verlis knew that this was at best a temporary distraction. He only hoped that it would provide him enough time to warn the workers at the mining operation that what they had feared most had happened.

Wings pounding the air, Verlis soared over the ancient home of the Dragons of Old, desperate to reach his human comrades in time. He flew low above the mages' encampment, finding it deserted as expected. Most of the workers would still be toiling at the mines, and he redoubled his speed, hurrying toward them. The mages were excavating dangerously close to the burial grounds of his ancestors, but he had kept them away from the actual graves of the ancient dragons.

The air was filled with the droning, grinding noise of the digging machine Timothy Cade had designed, and as Verlis swooped down toward the mining operation, he saw the metal thing burrowing into the hillside, boring a hole from which the mages would excavate tons of Malleum for weapons and armor to fight against the Wurm.

Or, at least, that had been the plan.

Time had suddenly run out.

Verlis caught sight of Walter Telford, the project coordinator, who stood talking animatedly with a pair of miners. They all wore troubled expressions, and Verlis understood. They wouldn't know yet that an attack was under way, but they were suffused with magic—they would have felt the magical matrix flicker.

"Walter!" the Wurm roared, smoke furling from his nostrils, the wind whipping past him.

Telford glanced up and lifted a hand. "Greetings, Verlis," he cried over the sounds of the digging machine. "I see you felt it as well. Do you have any idea—"

"The Divide has fallen!" the Wurm bellowed over the noise of the excavation, streams of fire leaking from his jaws.

Telford stepped back, the look upon his face showing that he wasn't sure he had heard correctly. The coordinator's eyes bulged as he turned to another worker, saying something into his ear. The worker ran to stand beneath the Burrower, waving his arms to shut the noisy machine down.

"Are you sure, Verlis?" Telford called. As the site fell silent, all mining operations ceasing, the men and women gathered around. "Absolutely certain?"

"I saw the barrier fall with my own eyes," the Wurm growled. "Whatever interrupted the flow of magic gave Raptus and his sorcerers the opening they needed. Alhazred's Divide has been torn down. The Wurm of Draconae are invading!"

The coordinator's body seemed to diminish in size, his head slowly hanging low. "We're not ready. There are no weapons, no armor, except what's at the Forge right now."

From the distance came a sound that could have been the rumbling of a distant storm, but Verlis knew otherwise.

Telford heard it as well, craning his head to listen. The others began to mutter worriedly, some already starting to move away from the machine and the mine, searching for some kind of cover. In the distance Verlis saw the workers from the Forge, wearing their heavy gloves and thick aprons, begin to emerge from the building where the Malleum was being processed.

"That's not a storm, is it?" Telford asked, looking up and out of the valley at the slate gray sky.

"No, it is not," Verlis replied, his inner fire roiling within his chest, causing steam to rise from the sides of his mouth. The sound was moving closer.

"Come on, all of you!" Telford shouted, and he started at a run toward the Forge.

Many of the miners followed, but others took that as their signal to flee in earnest. Instead of hurrying away, they were sprinting, perhaps thinking to take shelter in some cave or other. None of them ran toward the village. It would be in flames soon enough.

Verlis took flight, keeping pace with Telford and the miners courageous enough not to run for their lives. The Wurm glanced back repeatedly, and he saw dark figures against the sky, Raptus's soldiers at last taking flight. Black smoke rose on the horizon, the first of the huts now burning in the small village encampment the mages had built.

Telford led them to the Forge. The workers there were all moving outside, curiosity and fear etched in their faces. Verlis saw Charna Tayvis, the Forge supervisor, but her focus was on Telford.

"What's going on, Walter?" Charna demanded. She was a large, powerful-looking woman, her face covered in the dirt and grime of her labors. The blacksmiths grumbled behind her, eager for an answer as well.

"We're under attack. Raptus has broken through."

The blacksmiths looked horrified, as well they should have. Raptus was a brutal savage and a cunning general, utterly without mercy. Verlis knew this from experience. But Telford did not allow fear to fester.

"Gather up whatever you've already forged, Malleum weapons, helmets, whatever there is," he instructed the smiths. "Not a piece is to be wasted."

Charna stepped forward, removing the heavy gloves from her hands. "A good many pieces were shipped out to Arcanum two days past," she said. "Enough to fortify a battalion. All that's left here is what we've worked on since then."

One of the miners, the man who had been operating Timothy's digging machine, came forward. Fear shone in his eyes, and Verlis could smell the stink of panic seeping from his pores.

"And what then?" he asked, gazing up toward the rim of

the small valley in which they toiled. The rumbling was louder now—closer. "Once we gather the weapons—what then?"

One of the blacksmiths had left the Forge carrying a weapon he had obviously been working on. It was a Malleum spear, its head tapering to a nasty point. Forged from this metal, it would pierce even the toughest of Wurm hides, and their armor as well.

Telford took the weapon from him and hefted it in his hands. "We use them for what they were intended," he said in a forceful voice, eyes searching out every face in the crowd. "We use them to fight for our lives."

Miners and smiths alike dispersed quickly, rushing into the Forge to arm themselves.

"How long before they are upon us?" Telford asked, coming to stand at Verlis's side, spear still in hand.

"Not long," Verlis growled, watching the sky begin to darken with black smoke as the entire village was set aflame. Ominous winged figures cruised amid the smoke, the flapping of hundreds of pairs of wings sounding like the roll of thunder. "Not long at all."

Timothy knelt by the body of Leander Maddox, his friend and mentor, who had looked out for him since the death of his father. The mage had been a huge man both in stature and in heart, but he seemed so small now, there on the ground, no life left within him, no spirit, no magic. Cassandra had gone quickly back up to the room from which they had descended into this secret chamber and brought back the lantern of hungry fire that Timothy used. This, to him, was pure fire. Not magical. Not ghostfire, made from the souls of dead mages. This world had always perceived it as the rechanneling of magical energy to useful purpose, but Timothy had discovered that the ghosts of mages were trapped in the fire, unable to go on to their final reward, and he thought it criminally tragic.

Now Cassandra knelt by his side, hungry fire lantern in her hand, and shared in his sorrow over the death of the man who had been their teacher and protector. Not far away stood Ivar, last surviving warrior of the Asura tribe. He had suffered injuries in the battle with Alhazred, but he stood with his hands together as though saying a prayer over Leander's remains, and he muttered a kind of incantation under his breath, a chant to some higher power.

Cassandra placed the lantern on the floor beside him. "I'm so sorry," she said, bowing her head. "I knew him only a short time, but long enough to know he was a great man. Arcanum has lost a treasure today."

"He will be missed," Ivar said, his voice raspy and weak. "More than ever, the Parliament of Mages needs leaders like Leander Maddox."

Timothy heard their words of solace, but could not find his own voice. His mind was filled with memories of the man, of the kindness in his eyes, of the quiet strength that he had and that he inspired in others. Timothy recalled the first time he had seen Leander as he came through the magical doorway from Terra and into the world where the boy had been hidden away at birth due to his *affliction*. Even then, at that first look, he had known that the burly, bearded mage with the wild mane of red hair was a friend. Leander had been manipulated by evil, but in his heart, he had always remained loyal to the memory of Timothy's father, Argus Cade, who had been Leander's own teacher.

With a long, mournful breath, Timothy finally summoned the words in his heart. He held Leander's cold, stiff fingers in his own. "He always felt responsible, somehow, for the way the mages treated me. He blamed himself for their fear, their ignorance. I was born on Terra, but I think he wished that he had left me where he'd found me—to spare me from all that I've been exposed to since stepping through that doorway into this world."

Timothy studied Leander's pale face. If not for the spatters of blood that dappled the man's cheek, it would have appeared that the great mage was merely sleeping.

Cassandra put a comforting hand on his shoulder.

"He couldn't have been more wrong," Timothy said. "Sure, there are times when I wish I could run back to Patience and hide, but then I think about all I'd be giving up. My island home seems so . . . insignificant after seeing what exists beyond it."

He felt a wave of emotion threaten to reduce him to tears, but held it temporarily at bay. "You opened my eyes to wonders that existed beyond the doorway, Leander, and for that I will always love and miss you terribly."

Leaning forward, he placed a kiss on the man's brow and

climbed to his feet, still fighting to not be overpowered by grief. He felt Cassandra and Ivar's concerned eyes on him, but only nodded to confirm that he would be all right.

Across the vast chamber, a tapestry adorned with the crest of the Order of Alhazred hung on the wall. Timothy went over and tore it down from the place where it had likely hung for centuries. As he crossed the room with the tapestry, he made a promise to himself that he would not suppress his grief forever, that he would give himself time to truly mourn the passing of his friend, but for the moment there were things to be dealt with that had to take priority over his anguish.

"Tim?" Cassandra asked. "Are you all right?"

"Not even close," he said, draping the tapestry over Leander's still form. "But now that the horror of Alhazred's schemes is done with, I will be. Everything will be better now. It has to be. Leander died to make it so."

He said a silent good-bye to Leander, then went to Ivar, whose face masked the pain he must have been in after the conflict with Alhazred. The dark wizard had drained some of Ivar's spirit, and it would take time for him to recover. As a child on the Island of Patience, Ivar had been his friend, and as great a teacher to him then as Leander would later become. All his life his friends had looked out for him. Now it was time for Timothy to return the favor.

"Let's get you to a healer," Timothy said. "And then we need to let the others know what happened here today."

Cassandra nodded in agreement, picking up the lantern

from the floor to light their way up the stairs that led to a storage room where the secret passage to Alhazred's hidden lair was first discovered.

It seemed as though it took three times as long to climb the stairs as it had to descend them, and Timothy spent this time pondering the future of the Parliament of Mages and the world of Terra. Yes, Alhazred had been destroyed, but that did little to squelch the fear that he harbored over the potential threat of invasion from Draconae. Timothy shivered as he recalled his time in the Wurm world as Raptus's prisoner.

"We're almost there, Ivar," Timothy said, helping support his friend as they made their ascent of the winding stone staircase.

As they rounded a corner, a large shape was silhouetted in the doorway above them, and a bird fluttered over it. In the midst of his pain, Timothy found a spark of comfort at the sight, for the silhouette was that of Sheridan, the mechanical man he had built, with Edgar, the black-feathered rook who had been his father's familiar. Timothy was no mage, but Edgar was his familiar now.

"Caw! Caw!" Edgar cried. "It's them! By the tail feathers of my ancestors, it's them!"

"Timothy! You're alive!" Sheridan said, extending his segmented metal arms down the staircase to assist them in their climb. He clanked as he moved, and steam hissed from the release valve on the side of his head.

Another day, Timothy might have made a joke of Sheridan's

pointing out the obvious, but there was nothing amusing in the mechanical man's concern for him. Not all those who had descended into the belly of SkyHaven to combat Alhazred were coming back alive.

Cassandra went first, with the lantern, and then Timothy helped Ivar through the door into the storage chamber, barraged by questions from their anxious friends. There were half a dozen mages in the room, acolytes of the Order of Alhazred, but though Cassandra was their grandmaster, as a sign of respect they would stay away from Timothy unless they were forced to confront him.

"Thank Zephyrus you're safe," said Caiaphas, the navigation mage who had served Leander long and well. Those who had studied that specialty all wore a distinctive veil that covered most of their faces, leaving only their eyes visible, but Timothy could see the relief in him. He could almost not bear to meet that gaze.

Caiaphas frowned and peered back down into the darkness of the stairwell. "But where is Master Leander?"

"Yeah," Edgar croaked, tucking his wings back and tilting his head, looking down from his perch on Sheridan's shoulder. "Where is he? Guarding Alhazred or—"

They all then saw the look on Timothy's face, and their expressions tore at his heart. *Just let me be strong now,* he thought. *Just let me be strong for my friends.*

"Alhazred is truly dead now," he said. "But Leander . . . if not for him arriving when he did, none of us would have made it out of there alive. But the cost . . . ," Timothy said, prying the terrible words from his mouth. "Leander was killed."

They were all thunderstruck, each of them falling silent. Caiaphas closed his eyes and turned away, hanging his head. Edgar fluttered his wings, beak opening as though trying to find something to say. Sheridan's glowing red eyes dimmed and his arms hung at his sides as though he had shut himself down. The other Alhazred mages muttered among themselves, some of them gazing at Timothy with open suspicion.

"What went on down there, kid?" Edgar asked at last, flapping his wings as he flew up to a new perch atop Sheridan's head. "It must've been awful. The whole place started falling. We thought it was the end for all of us."

"It was terrifying," the mechanical man agreed. "How can such a thing happen, that spells so powerful and intricate could falter?"

The acolytes watched Timothy with fear in their eyes, as if they knew that he was somehow responsible. The un-magician was to blame.

And they were right.

"It was Alhazred," Timothy began. "By absorbing the soul energies in the ghostfire, he managed to connect himself to the magical matrix. He was draining it, making himself stronger and stronger. He was going to try to take control of the whole thing, to command all the magic in the world. Leander tried to stop him, but Alhazred was too strong. If I hadn't done what I did . . ."

"What did you do, Timothy?" the black bird asked in a troubled whisper.

"I . . . I touched the matrix," he explained. "I touched the matrix and for a moment, I think I might have shut it down."

The mages huddled together, whispering among themselves. The suspicion in them had turned to utter terror at the very thought of such a thing.

"Oh, dear," Sheridan muttered.

"You sure did something, kid," Edgar said. "For a minute there I thought the whole place was going into the drink."

Timothy looked around at the shambles the room had become, shelves fallen over and debris scattered across the floor. "Is everybody all right?" he asked. "Is SkyHaven all right?"

"Other than the mess, everything appears to be fine now," Caiaphas replied. "But, Timothy, it was not just Sky-Haven that was affected. For a moment we all felt our magic leave us."

His head swam with the enormity of what he had done. He had no idea that he could be capable of such a feat, and for a brief moment, he was actually afraid of himself.

"Timothy did what was necessary," Cassandra said, her voice filled with authority and gravity. As it should have been, for with Leander's demise, she was the one, true Grandmaster of the order now. "If not for him, Alhazred would have been unstoppable." She looked about the chamber, making certain that all were listening. "Without Timothy, we would all be enslaved to Alhazred now, all of our magic in his control."

Cassandra turned to one of the acolytes. "Take Ivar to the physician at once," she ordered.

The mage bowed at the waist, then carefully approached the Asura warrior. Ivar hesitated, looking to Timothy.

"Don't worry, old friend," Timothy said. "I'll be fine until you get back."

Ivar nodded once, and allowed himself to be led from the chamber. No sooner had they departed than Carlyle, personal assistant to the Grandmaster, charged into the room, several more acolytes in tow.

"Thank the gods," he said, placing a hand to his chest. Carlyle was normally fussy and derisive, but in the midst of this crisis he had proven himself a valuable ally . . . and revealed himself to have once been a combat mage. "When SkyHaven began to fall, I thought the worst."

He paused for a moment, carefully studying their number, and frowned. "What of Grandmaster Maddox?"

Timothy couldn't bear to explain it all again, and was grateful when Caiaphas took charge.

"My master fell during the battle with Alhazred," he explained. "I go now to recover his body." The navigation mage turned, moving toward the stairs.

Carlyle's face tightened with pain. He gritted his teeth and seemed to deflate. "Caiaphas," he said, following after the navigation mage, "please allow the order to assist you." He gestured toward the acolytes, and several quickly followed Caiaphas into the secret passage.

"What a dark day," Carlyle added, almost as though he were speaking to himself.

Timothy had always found Carlyle annoying, but during

the crisis of the past few days, he had begun to see a different side to the man. There was much more to the Grandmaster's assistant than he had originally believed.

Now Carlyle composed himself, pushing aside his sorrow the way one would remove a cloak, and proceeded to report to Cassandra. He told her of the shipment of Malleum weapons the parliamentary headquarters had received earlier that morning from Tora'nah, and explained that SkyHaven's sudden lurch in the sky had made a mess, but not caused any serious structural damage. At least none that the inspectors could find.

Only half listening to Carlyle's report, Timothy took notice of a spider as it crawled across the chamber floor, and he was immediately reminded of an evil among them.

"What about Grimshaw?"

"Don't worry about that lunatic," Edgar croaked. "Security made sure he stayed put when the magic blinked out, and last I checked, he was still locked away tight."

"Where, I might add, he belongs," Sheridan said, punctuating his words with a toot of steam.

But Timothy kept his focus on Carlyle, wanting official word.

The serious little man nodded toward Edgar. "Indeed, former constable Grimshaw remains confined to a holding cell, awaiting prosecution for his crimes."

Timothy breathed a sigh of relief, hoping now for a moment of respite to collect his thoughts and mourn the loss of his friend. All too soon he would discover that it was simply the calm before a storm.

Carlyle stopped to compose himself before entering the chamber where Lord Romulus of the Legion Nocturne awaited a word with him.

Conjuring a looking glass, he studied his reflection, dismayed at the circles beneath his eyes and the lack of color on his lips. There could be no rest for the personal assistant to the Grandmaster of the Order of Alhazred. It was his duty to be sure that everything ran smoothly, and to do that meant a certain amount of sacrifice. Sacrifice and discipline, both things he had learned a great deal about as a combat mage, many years ago.

His mind raced with thoughts of all that had happened these past months—since the arrival of the Cade boy. It was both amazing and terrifying so much could change upon the appearance of one individual. If someone had told him that all of Arcanum—no, all the world—would be thrown into turmoil with the introduction of a single child, he would have laughed out loud and called them mad.

But it has happened, he mused, staring at his reflection in the shimmering surface. Timothy's return to Terra seemed to have been the catalyst for change, forcing the world around them down a frightening new path to the unknown.

Carlyle had yet to decide if this was a good thing.

He waved his hand in the air, dispersing the magical mirror as if it were made of smoke. Now was not the time for such rumination. Now was the time to do his appointed job—to make certain everything functioned as it was supposed to at

SkyHaven, or at least to create the appearance of such.

"Lord Romulus," Carlyle said with a bow as the double doors opened into the chamber. "So sorry to keep you waiting, things today have been a tad . . . chaotic."

The Grandmaster of the Legion Nocturne had been standing out on the balcony, and now turned at the sound of Carlyle's voice. The armored giant was a fearsome sight.

"What is going on here, sir?" Romulus bellowed, clenching and unclenching his large hands, covered in studded gloves of dark leather. "Who's in charge here? What's become of the boy, and of Maddox? And what of the . . . flickering . . . of the matrix?"

The leader of the Legion Nocturne looked down on him, and Carlyle gazed up into the eyes that glowered from inside the darkness of the great horned helmet Romulus wore.

"I felt it, as I am certain we all did," Romulus continued. "My sky carriage began to fall toward the sea, and as it did, I saw SkyHaven dropping. . . ."

Romulus moved even closer and Carlyle could smell the almost animal aroma that exuded from the body of the fearsome man.

"I have felt this . . . loss . . . before, Carlyle. When Timothy Cade touched me. I demand an explanation."

Carlyle felt a claw of dread grip his heart. *I touched the magical matrix,* the boy had said. Timothy's . . . affliction had always made Carlyle apprehensive, but this was something altogether different—and profoundly disturbing.

"Ah yes, that," he said, struggling to keep his voice calm. "I believe the Cade boy was responsible, extending his unique *talents* to prevent Alhazred from enslaving us all."

Romulus reared back as if Carlyle had tried to strike him. "Extended his talents?" he snarled, his voice echoing from within the helmet. "Do you understand what you're saying?"

Carlyle wasn't positive, but he could have sworn he heard a trace of fear in the Nocturne Grandmaster's question.

"Quite," he replied, carefully. "But Cassandra—that is, Grandmaster Nicodemus, has said that if the boy hadn't done so, Alhazred would have—"

"He touched the matrix," Romulus interrupted, grabbing hold of Carlyle's robes and drawing him closer. "The Cade boy's insidious powers traveled beyond the walls of SkyHaven—who knows how far?"

Carlyle caused a charge of magical energy to course through his body and Romulus grunted as a blue spark of energy forced him to remove his hands from the assistant's clothing.

"I understand your concern, Grandmaster Romulus," Carlyle stated, brushing the wrinkles from his front. "But Timothy Cade acted in defense of us all, and so far there have been no reports of any serious repercussions."

As if to make a liar of him, the air began to shimmer between them, and the face of Alethea Borgia, the Voice of Parliament, appeared in their midst. Her expression in that magical communiqué was severe.

"Lord Romulus!" the Voice snapped.

The gigantic Legion Grandmaster inclined his head respectfully. "At your service."

"Alhazred's Divide has fallen," the Voice stated, stumbling over the last word as though she could hardly believe what she was reporting. "The Wurm have come through and are now attacking our operations at Tora'nah."

Romulus glared at Carlyle. "You were saying?"

CHAPTER TWO

Wurm dropped from the sky, wings beating the air unmercifully, gouts of orange flame streaming from their mouths as they laid waste the mages' mining operations in Tora'nah.

Verlis tensed, struggling with the urge to throw himself into battle, but he had made a pledge to himself to do everything in his power to keep Walter Telford and his people safe. They were hiding inside a wooden storage shed used to house the various supplies needed to run the Forge. The scent of the black heatstone, volcanite, hung heavy in the air.

"What are we going to do?" one of the smiths asked. He was the youngest of the metal workers.

No one answered, and then Verlis realized that they were waiting for *him* to respond. "We can't stay here," he said with a growl, peering out through a crack in the door.

The raiders outside were in a frenzy, destroying everything in their path, and he could hear the screams of the dying, of mages who had been in the village or in an area of the mining operation too far from Telford's core crew and hadn't found anywhere to hide. Ordinary mages had basic magic at their disposal, but were not trained for fighting. The average Wurm also had rudimentary magical skills, but Wurm spent their entire lives preparing for war. There was no question how this day would end.

"It is only a matter of time before they find us," Verlis said with a growl. He turned to look at those who had followed him when the invasion began. In addition to Telford and Charna, there were perhaps fifteen blacksmiths and miners gathered in that cramped space. They had retrieved as many weapons and pieces of armor as they could carry, and it all rested in a heap on the floor behind them.

"Do you think we could make it to the sky carriages?" Charna asked, her eyes wide in terror. "Perhaps even save some of the others?"

Verlis shook his head, smoke furling from his nostrils. "Raptus's elite would burn us from the sky before we had a chance to clear the valley."

A stream of Wurm fire dropped dangerously close to the shack in which they hid, and they could feel the intense heat of the flames that now burned the very soil.

"What then?" Telford asked. "Those who were quickest into the fray have shown us the foolishness of trying to fight. If we had greater numbers, perhaps, but hearing their screams and watching them burn has shown us the truth. We are no match for Raptus and his army. Do we just wait here to die? I would rather rush out to meet my fate, to have a more noble death."

Verlis returned to the door and again gazed out on the devastation of the encampment. To remain here was certain death, but what if they did make their way from the valley? Would their chances be any better then?

"All right. You must listen to me," he said, returning his attention to the smiths and miners. "What I am about to propose may sound like madness, but I fear it is our only chance. Unless, friend Walter, you insist upon discarding your life needlessly?"

"Go on," Telford encouraged. "Any chance of living is better than dying at the mercy of those monsters."

The others nodded in agreement.

"Wearing what armor and weapons remain, we will fight our way out of the valley, to the one place Raptus's villains will not follow."

"You're insane," one of the smiths spat, a large man with a long, black beard on which he nervously tugged. "What chance do we have against those . . . those things?"

"More than if you wait for them to find you here," the Wurm explained, two trails of steam drifting from his nostrils, as the flame inside him began to churn with anticipation. "Our object is to survive long enough to reach our goal, not to be victorious."

"You have courage and honor, Verlis, but perhaps too

much faith in us," Telford said. "And where could we go that they wouldn't follow? Eventually they would . . ."

The project coordinator's voice trailed off, and his eyes lit with understanding. "You can't possibly be suggesting—"

Verlis stretched his wings as far as he could within the confines of the shed. "I am. The one place we might flee that the other Wurm will not follow. Alhazred's Divide has fallen. The way is open for us to cross into Draconae. All the Wurm serving Raptus are here now, and they would never return there for fear that they would become trapped again."

Charna swore under her breath. "You're correct, Verlis. It is madness."

"It is our only hope," the Wurm said. "We make our escape to Draconae. Once removed from the immediate threat of Raptus and his legions, we can begin to plot our return to Arcanum."

The sound of crackling fire and the thunder of beating wings drew closer, and Verlis knew they were only moments from discovery.

"We need to act now," he urged.

The smiths and miners eyed one another nervously.

"It's a simple question, lads," Telford spoke to them. "Either you take a chance on living, or you resign yourselves to die. What will it be?"

The group remained silent, and then it was the burly, bearded man who showed Verlis the decision they had silently made. He went to the pile of armor and weapons, rummaging through the heavy metal objects until he found the helmet they had forged for Verlis.

"We had hoped to polish it up some before returning it to you," he said, handing it to the Wurm. "Perhaps we will still get the chance."

Verlis took it and placed it upon his head, horns sliding easily through the holes that had been made for them. "My thanks," he growled as they began to dress themselves in the armor, choosing weapons.

The building shook as the invaders soared overhead. They were closer now—dangerously so. There came a chorus of roars and the stink of sulfur as the roof of the building was set ablaze, fire rippling across the ceiling.

"Do not panic. Steel yourselves," Charna instructed them.

The smiths and miners stood ready, clad in armor and armed with weapons made from the Malleum they had extracted from the ground and forged to fight the Wurm. What they couldn't wear, they carried in makeshift packs on their backs. No Malleum was to be wasted. When they at last made their way back to Arcanum, it would be given to combat mages who would help repel the enemy.

Verlis flexed his powerful wings. "Are you ready?" His clawed hand rested on the door latch.

"Ready for combat? Not one of us, my friend. But we're not ready to die, either," Walter replied as he dropped the helmet visor down to shield his eyes. He turned to the others and raised his weapon in salute. They responded in kind.

★ ★ ★

Timothy stared at Carlyle, heart heavy with guilt. "I'm responsible . . . aren't I?" He sat down heavily in a chair in the Grandmaster's office, burying his face in his hands.

"No one can say for certain," Carlyle answered. "But it does appear rather likely."

"I'm just what Parliament feared I was," he said. "A menace. A danger to the world."

"I'll hear none of that," Cassandra scolded, standing up from the large, high-backed chair behind the expanse of rich dark wood that had been Leander's desk. *Her* desk, now. "The fall of the Divide was just an unforeseen side effect of your defeat over Alhazred. You had no way of knowing it would happen."

Edgar ruffled his wings as he strolled across the top of the desk. "She's got you there, kid."

Timothy raised his head from his hands. "Unforeseen side effect?" he repeated in disbelief. "I'm responsible for allowing a Wurm invasion into the world." He stood and began to pace. "Don't you think you're downplaying the enormity of what I've done just a bit?"

"Now, Timothy," Sheridan said in a soothing voice. The mechanical man had been standing by Cassandra's desk, but now took several clanking steps forward, red eyes flaring brightly. "Getting upset won't do you, or anybody else, a bit of good. What's done is done."

Timothy approached the window, but not so close as to cancel out the enchantment of the shimmering spell-glass that filled its frame. "I'm a danger to this world." He stared out at the churning sea below the floating fortress. "It would have been better for everyone if I'd never left Patience."

Someone approached him, and from the delicate scent of flowers that wafted in the air, he knew it was Cassandra.

"Don't talk like that," she chided him. "If you had not left Patience for Terra . . ."

Timothy turned to face her, staring into her beautiful green eyes. "Leander would still be alive, your grandfather would likely still be Grandmaster of the Order of Alhazred and Raptus and his Wurm legions would still be locked away in Draconae. Tell me that isn't better than what we have now."

She stared back defiantly. "My grandfather was an evil monster, serving an even fouler master, and you yourself told me that the Wurm had already been working on a way through Alhazred's Divide and were near to success. Leander's death shatters my heart, but he was already working with the Parliament to discover the truth about the disappearance of so many mages, and his investigation would have led him to Alhazred eventually. You don't know what fate would have brought without your participation."

Deep down, Timothy knew that she was right, but he couldn't shake the feeling of responsibility for the constant turmoil that had been threatening the world since he'd decided to make Terra his home.

"It's all so much," he whispered.

There came a sound like the disapproving clucking of a tongue, and then a voice spoke in their midst, the speaker unseen. "Have you forgotten all that I have tried to teach you?"

Only Carlyle seemed startled. The others were all used to the Asura's ability to blend with his surroundings, to change the pigment of his skin so much that he seemed to be invisible.

"Ivar," Timothy said, a spark of hope rising in him. If nothing else, at least his friend and teacher was all right. "I haven't forgotten anything—at least I don't think I have."

As though he had suddenly been transported into the room, Ivar appeared. It was not magic, however. Or, at least, not the sort the mages of Terra understood. The natural hue of Ivar's skin was pale, almost ivory, save for the inky black markings of his tribe. The marks were not tattoos, but generated from within, Ivar making the skin black in those spots, in those shapes, as a way to honor his past. Timothy was elated to see his friend up and around after all he had been through. At least something was going right.

"I can't imagine I'll ever get used to that," Carlyle muttered breathlessly.

"Tell you the truth," Edgar croaked from the desk, "you never really do."

Cassandra went to Ivar, a gentle smile on her face that reached her green eyes. "How are you, Ivar?" she asked. "Feeling better?"

The Asura nodded slowly, but never took his dark eyes

from Timothy. "I am feeling much better, Grandmaster," he said politely. "The healers of SkyHaven are quite skillful, but I am troubled by what I have just heard."

Ivar stared at Timothy. "You say you have not forgotten my teaching, but the words that come from your mouth—they are not words spoken by an Asura."

Timothy turned his gaze away from his teacher, and friend. "I don't understand," he lied.

Ivar's gaze seem to bore into him, attempting to push him back, but Timothy held his ground. "You have come quite far in mastering the fighting techniques of my people."

"He's become quite the scrapper, if I do say so myself," Sheridan chimed in, gears noisily grinding from inside his metal body. He held up his fists, pretending to do combat with the air.

"But that's not what you're talking about, is it?" Timothy asked, an anger building up inside him that was aimed at himself more than anyone, and yet he found himself turning it against his friends.

"When I entered this room, I heard a boy filled with self-pity, ready to give in to the forces that assault him." Ivar slowly shook his head. "That is not the way of the Asura."

Timothy remembered all that he'd been taught. Even now the words echoed through his mind and images rose in him of long days on the beaches of Patience, the sky orange with afternoon sunlight, his muscles aching from the combat training Ivar had given him.

"An Asura does not hide from life, he embraces both the

good and the bad," Timothy said, remembering.

Ivar nodded, black patterns flowing across the muscular surface of his pale flesh. "Nothing may change what has already happened, all that remains is the response."

Timothy sighed, feeling the weight of all that had happened to him attempting to drive him to his knees. "It's so much," he repeated, seeking some level of sympathy from the warrior, but knowing it was not likely to come.

"And how will you respond?" Ivar asked. "Will it dominate, or will you show it who is master?"

Timothy took a deep breath, and in his mind he returned once more to the Island of Patience. To the beach. To Ivar's teachings. And suddenly it was all so clear. The world was in peril—the world that he had decided to make his own. Timothy was the un-magician, and there were things he could do that no one else in this whole world was capable of. That had to count for something.

"You're right, Ivar. I've wasted enough time feeling sorry for myself." Grim-faced, he turned toward Cassandra and Carlyle, a rush of adrenaline coursing through his body. "If the Wurm have broken through, I need to get to my father's estate and talk with Verlis's clan. If anybody can tell us how to deal with Raptus, it's them."

Edgar cawed and took flight, beating his wings in the confines of the room and flying in a circle just beneath the ceiling. "Now that's more like it!"

Sheridan crossed his arms with a clank and a hiss of steam from the valve on the side of his head. There was little range in his facial expressions, but Timothy was sure he saw pride and satisfaction in the mechanical man's face.

When he looked at Cassandra, though—at the girl whose beauty and bravery stole his breath away—he saw regret. She brushed a lock of her long red hair out of her face, tucking it behind her ear.

"I am the Grandmaster now," she said. "The order is in disarray. Leander is dead, but so is Alhazred. It remains to be seen if there is even an order for me to lead, and if so, if any of us can bear to keep the name of the monster as the mark of our guild. In any case, there are hundreds of mages in service to the Order of Alhazred in Sunderland alone. They must all be summoned to join the fight against Raptus. Carlyle and I must stay here to muster those forces and try to determine the future of the order."

Timothy gazed at her. With all the heartache of recent days, what he felt for Cassandra was the one bright spot. She was a year or two older than he was, but the electricity between them was undeniable. When all of this was done, when destiny was content to let them rest awhile, he wanted nothing more than to see what would become of that bond. But for now, they both had responsibilities. Still, he couldn't bear the idea of anything happening to her.

"I understand. But I'd like Ivar to stay here with you, to give you his aid and counsel, if he would agree."

Ivar bowed. "As you wish," he said. And there was something in his eyes that said he understood exactly what Timothy was thinking.

Within the central spire of the Xerxis, the headquarters of the Parliament of Mages, the great hall buzzed like an angry swarm of stingers on the final day of summer. *The sound of panic,* Lord Romulus mused as he walked about the grand chamber, observing the frenzied chatter of the grandmasters of the 167 other guilds.

A sound of desperation.

Romulus grew impatient. The other grandmasters sensed his dangerously foul mood and would not dare to interrupt his pacing, but he himself wished for some distraction. They were all awaiting the arrival of their *Voice.*

They did not have much longer to wait.

Alethea Borgia, the Voice of Parliament, emerged from her private office and strode into the center of that circular chamber, her staff clutched tightly in her hand. The polished bone gleamed in the flickering light of ghostfire lamps. Romulus noticed that the white-haired woman was wearing robes of dark, angry red as opposed to her usual tranquil colors. The Voice was adorned in the color of war.

The Voice struck her staff three times on the floor, indicating that it was time for their assembly to commence. But the members of Parliament did not listen, deaf to Alethea's attempts to silence their frantically waving tongues.

Rage churned in Romulus's heart, rage over the dark twist fate had taken, rage over the ignorance shown by his peers, and rage at all of them, himself included, for believing that the Wurm could be betrayed and banished without fear of reprisal.

"Silence!" he bellowed, his booming voice echoing throughout the chamber, causing the chatter of the frenzied throng to cease in an instant.

Lord Foxheart of the Malleus Guild shot Romulus a dark look, his rodentlike features twitching to expose his sharp, pointy teeth. But Foxheart held his tongue, perhaps sensing that this was not the day to challenge the Grandmaster of the Legion Nocturne.

"I am the Voice of Parliament," the silver-haired woman said, her voice not as loud as Romulus's, but twice as authoritative. "And our community has been called together this day for reasons most dire."

She looked about, her gaze touching upon each and every member of Parliament. Romulus respectfully bowed his head, heavy with black metal helm.

"Our world has been invaded," she went on, her voice rife with emotion. "Alhazred's Divide has fallen. The Wurm are here."

Dozens of grandmasters leaped to their feet, frenzied demands and suggestions streaming from their mouths. Grandmaster Arcturus Tot of the Palisades Guild tried to shout his opinion over the voice of Mistress Belladonna of the Order of Strychnos. Lord Foxheart shouted all the louder to be heard over the rants and raves of the representatives of the Drayaidi, Winter Star, and Sectus guilds.

Romulus was about to scream at them to hold their tongues yet again, when the Voice of Parliament raised her arms high and the head of her bone staff crackled with a blue light that formed an undulating cloud of magical power. It writhed and pulsated in the air above their heads, high up in the center of the tower. Whiplike tendrils reached down from the cloud, touching each member—stealing away their voices.

The great hall was plunged into silence, and Romulus smiled within the darkness of his helmet, untouched by the spell storm, for he knew when it was best to hold his tongue.

"Your voices shall be returned to you when I deem that you have earned the right to use them again for the benefit of your guilds," the Voice of Parliament proclaimed. "But for now, I turn our discussion over to the Parliament's Master of Arms, High Lord Romulus of the Legion Nocturne."

The Voice pointed her staff of bone at him as he descended from his row to stand in the circle beside her.

Romulus looked up at the gathered mages, marveling at the fact that many of the grandmasters still were attempting to speak, even though their mouths had been silenced.

He turned toward the Voice and bowed. "Kind thoughts to you this most troubling of days," Romulus grumbled.

"On this and all days," she replied with a bow of her own. "Will you speak to us of our defense, and how we will rid our world of this heinous threat?"

"I will," he replied, turning to face his silent audience. "Kind thoughts to you all," he said, not expecting the traditional response, given the circumstances. "Our world is under attack, and it is time for us to decide how we will react."

The grandmasters had at last begun to pay attention. Most of them returned to their seats in the Parliamentary chamber.

"As you are all aware, we were warned that such an attack could be coming. Timothy Cade has been to Draconae and brought back a clan of Wurm who returned to this world because they were being exterminated by the followers of the tyrant Raptus. With Verlis, head of that clan, the Cade boy brought word that Raptus was a hate-filled, merciless creature, and that he was attempting to shatter the Divide and invade. They want vengeance for the injustices done to their people."

Romulus watched the faces of the members of Parliament. Many of them scowled at the mention of the Cade boy. Once, Romulus would have reacted the same way, but the un-magician had more than proven his courage. Timothy was an extremely controversial subject on the floor of Parliament. The boy scared them, and rightfully so, but he just may have been their best hope for dealing with this threat.

"Timothy helped to create a tenuous truce between the Parliament of Mages and Verlis's clan, and so we have Wurm allies in our impending war against Raptus's army. But here is the question. Can we put our trust in this boy, invisible to the matrix? Do we trust Timothy Cade with what could very well be the fate of our world?"

The members of Parliament were on their feet in a heartbeat, waving their arms and wailing silently.

"Perhaps it is time to give them back their voices," Romulus suggested to Alethea Borgia. "They should be allowed to express their opinions."

The Voice raised her bone staff, whispered something Romulus could not hear, and a rumble filled the great hall. This was one of the powers unique to the Voice of Parliament and none of them could combat it. Now, though, the churning cloud of magical energy was dispersed.

"The power of speech is yours once more, my friends, but I will not hesitate to deprive you of it again if this debate is not conducted in an orderly fashion."

The grandmasters heeded the Voice's warning, glancing about respectfully. There was a hierarchy of power and seniority, based on how long each had served as grandmaster, and they observed that hierarchy now. After a moment Grandmaster Aloysius of the Spiral Guild stood.

"How can we possibly trust the boy?" he demanded. The man was rotund and red faced with anger. "Son of Argus Cade he may be, but he is not a part of our world. He was raised on a parallel plane, no more one of us than the Wurm themselves."

Aloysius looked around for support. Many of the members nodded in agreement, urging him on, some clearly impatient to have their own turn to speak. "The boy has thwarted us at every turn. He was responsible for the death of one of our most illustrious grandmasters, and broke a Wurm criminal free from the prison of Abbadon. It is a pity that the Parliament acted so harshly with Constable

Grimshaw, dismissing him from his duties, for he was correct. Timothy Cade and all he represents should be locked away, and the spell to free him forgotten."

A roar went up from the assemblage, each of them fighting to be noticed—to be recognized so they could have their moment. The Voice clacked her staff on the floor once, and they settled down somewhat, though the debate continued.

"Half truths at best," Romulus boomed. "Yes, at one time Grandmaster Nicodemus was a respected member of our Parliament. But there can be no denying that his true nature was abhorrent. He was a villain and a traitor and a murderer. And if not for the boy, we would never have learned the truth."

Mistress Belladonna of the Order of Strychnos rose from her seat, a striking and bewitchingly beautiful figure clad in robes of the most vibrant green, a barely noticeable glance to either side enough to quiet the mouths of the clamorous guild members seated around her.

"Lord Romulus, from your tone I take it that you believe we ought to trust Timothy Cade. Yet you have been one of the most vocal opponents of the boy. To what may we attribute such a change?"

Lord Foxheart leaped to his feet. "Isn't it obvious? The boy has clouded his mind!"

There were mocking chuckles from those who found the Malleus Guild's grandmaster absurd, but there were also grumbling nods of agreement from some members. Romulus had to restrain himself from the urge to reduce Foxheart to a pile of charred bones.

Instead he turned to the Voice. "May I show them?"

"I think we must," she replied, and passed her hand over the top of her bone staff. A crystalline shape twirled in the air, throwing colors as it reflected the light of the chamber.

With a gentle puff of her breath, the Voice sent the crystal drifting across the stage toward Romulus. He held his hand out, even as the crystal resolved into an image of fire, of Wurm raiders in flight, wielding swords and breathing liquid flame. Of slaughter and destruction.

"This is Tora'nah," Romulus announced.

The images were nightmarish to behold: an army of Wurm filling the sky, descending on the mining operation. And all the while the voice of a guild member could be heard. *"Help us, please help us."*

Then one of the Wurm warriors alighted on the ground just feet away from the mage who had recorded the frantic message. The creature was terrifying to behold, clad in pitted armor the color of dried blood. He opened his mouth as if to scream, spewing a stream of fire. A piercing shriek of agony filled the air, and the transmission went black.

The hall was deathly quiet as the crystal dissolved, raining down to the floor like so much dust.

"You ask me how I can trust the boy and his Wurm allies?" Romulus said. "After seeing such as this, how can I afford not to?"

CHAPTER THREE

T hey were slowing down.

And to slow down, Verlis knew, was to admit defeat and accept death.

The cold, biting winds of the Barrens swirled around them, kicking up razor-sharp slivers of ice that did little damage to his scaled hide, but left bleeding scratches on the exposed flesh of the surviving blacksmiths and miners of Tora'nah.

Fifteen had left the storage shed at the mining operation and raced for the portal between worlds, besieged by Raptus's vicious soldiers. The Wurm warriors had attacked with swords and fire, death on the wing, but as Verlis had predicted, they had all refused to re-enter Draconae. Still, the escape had been costly. Of the original fifteen, five had been killed before crossing over and two had died since then from wounds sustained during their exodus. Now only eight remained.

But even those eight were in peril from the unforgiving environment of Draconae, the wind and ice and the bone-deep chill. The night would be even worse.

"We must move faster," Verlis called to Telford over the howling winds.

The landscape of Draconae was cruel and inhospitable, ice barrens and mountains cloaked in constant blizzard, save in the areas where volcanic activity had burst up through the earth and created small oases of blistering tropical heat. Verlis wondered, as he often had while living on this cruel world, if the mages of old had chosen it intentionally, if they had secretly hoped in their blackened hearts that the place of banishment, now called Draconae, would eventually kill the Wurm. If that was indeed their intention, then the mages had not known their enemies well at all. For the Wurm were survivors, and this harsh land had only served to make them stronger, and in the case of Raptus and those who followed him, angrier.

Telford nodded in response to Verlis's urgings, pulling the collar of his jacket up around his neck. Ice and snow clung to his hair, and the man was shivering from the elements as he turned to the surviving workers.

"Come on, now," he yelled, his voice barely audible over the roar of the rushing winds. "We need to speed things up before . . ."

The smiths and miners slowed to a stop. What a ragtag group they made. The Malleum armor hung on their trembling frames as though they were children wearing their fathers' wares of war. Frost covered their features, and their breath froze almost before it could leave their blue-tinged lips.

"No farther," a burly smith cried out, stumbling forward to stand in front of the others, his head covered in ice and snow.

Verlis had learned that the man's name was Burtlett. He had been the assistant foreman at the metal forge, but would now be foreman. Charna Tayvis had been killed during the exodus from Tora'nah. She had been the first to fall, distracting Raptus's soldiers by running away from the group, goading the Wurm to pursue her while the others made their escape from the valley. Verlis had gained an entirely new respect for the human species, and their potential for sacrifice, this day—one that he would not soon forget.

"We're going back," Burtlett said, planting his spear into the frozen ground before him in defiance. "I've decided— *we've* decided that if we're going to die, we'd rather die back there, where it's warm."

Verlis noticed the other smiths and miners glancing nervously at one another, and had to wonder how much they had actually participated in making this decision.

They had all fought bravely. Though he himself had been engaged in savage combat with his brethren, Verlis had seen how valiantly the humans had waged their battle, even as they fled for their lives. The Malleum armor protected them from the razor-sharp points of swords, spears, and knives, and also deflected the spells the Wurm sorcerers cast against them. Now that he had borne witness to this, he had begun to believe that with the Malleum, the mages of Terra truly stood a chance against Raptus and his army. Fortunately much armor and weaponry would already have arrived in Arcanum from the earlier shipment. But every piece would be vital to the war effort. He had to get this dwindling group of survivors safely back to their world.

"No more of you will die," Verlis said, striding toward them. He pulled his wings tighter around his body to protect himself from the biting winds. "On the spirits of my ancestors, I promise you this."

"You're just as cold as we are," Burtlett argued. "You can't protect us from something that will eventually kill you as well."

Without a word Verlis stepped back, opened his mouth, and vomited a blazing gout of liquid flame onto the icy ground. The fire blazed, throwing off powerful warmth. The smiths and miners were drawn to the small conflagration, warming themselves, and seeming to take some inspiration from its invigorating heat. Though it made *him* colder, depleting his own inner warmth, Verlis knew that he had to give them hope.

"I will die before allowing the elements here to take you," he said with a growl. "To go back to the camp will surely mean your end."

The fire began to shrink, having nothing to burn, and he watched the mages huddle closer to the dwindling warmth. Soon it would be gone, and they would need to continue on.

"Stay with me and I will take you to a place where the walls between dimensions are thinner, where I can work the magic taught to me by one of your own—the most revered Argus Cade—and return you to your homeworld."

Telford moved to stand beside Verlis, a silent affirmation of his support. Burtlett glowered as one by one the others joined them.

"With me, there is a chance for life," the Wurm said to Burtlett, who continued to stand his ground. "Is that not more appealing than the alternative?"

At last the man grumbled beneath his breath, pulled his spear from the ground, and they all set off together across the frozen barren.

A great many Wurm soared in the sky above the Cade estate, adults and children roaring fire as they dipped and wove around the ancient structure. The house sprang from August Hill at the strangest of angles, only one corner of the house anchored to the ground, while the rest of it was supported by magic, dangling precariously over the hill with nothing below it but the gorgeous view of Arcanum. The mansion had suffered no evident structural damage in the flickering of the magical matrix, but as Caiaphas guided the sky carriage up August Hill, Timothy felt certain that many of the more delicate furnishings would have been shattered by the temporary jarring drop he had caused.

As the sky carriage approached, Timothy could not help but feel the wonder and excitement he had experienced the first time he laid eyes on the ancestral home of his family, the home that, in the wake of his father's death, belonged to him alone.

Home.

With amazing precision, the navigation mage brought the carriage to a stop at the end of the stone staircase that led down from the great doors of the house and ended over open air.

"It seems like such a long time since I was last here," Timothy said, pushing open the carriage door and stepping onto the stairs.

"If time were measured by experience, you have been away for a very long time indeed," Sheridan said as Timothy helped the mechanical man from the back of the carriage.

"Will you join us inside, Caiaphas?" Timothy asked as he closed the carriage door.

"I think I'll stay here, if you don't mind." The navigation mage gazed out over the sprawling city of Arcanum. "It's so peaceful right now." He paused a moment before continuing. "And who knows how long it will remain this way."

Timothy admired the city as well, trying hard not to think about what would happen if Raptus and his army attacked.

"That's fine," he told the driver. "But if you want to come inside, you're welcome."

Timothy went up the stairs, admiring the grandeur of his father's house. Sheridan clanked along behind him. There was the flutter of wings, and Timothy glanced up to see

Edgar spiraling down from the sky. The rook perched on his shoulder.

"Hello, Edgar," Timothy said. "Nice to stretch your wings, I'll bet."

The bird did not respond. His head was cocked back, beak pointed skyward as he gazed up at the roof of the house, where the Wurm were soaring and rolling in the air. Timothy thought he spotted Cythra, Verlis's mate.

"There's something you don't see every day," Edgar said.

Timothy smiled, happy to see the Wurm enjoying themselves. He only wished he did not have such terrible news. He reached the front door and stopped. Almost every door in the world had some form of magical lock to secure property and privacy, but those locks were useless to Timothy. The nullifying effect of his presence canceled out any security a spell would have provided. He might have left the existing spell-lock in place, but he did not trust magic. Instead he built his own lock. It was a simple invention, a metal bar placed across the door and frame on the inside, preventing the door from being opened. It took a key to slide that bar back, allowing the door to be opened.

"Do you have the key, Sheridan?" Timothy asked, extending his hand.

The mechanical man opened a small, hinged door in his chest and stuck his hand inside. "Certainly," he said, searching among the pumps, pistons, and gears that made up his internal workings. "It was right here the last time I looked . . . ah, here it is."

Sheridan withdrew the small, cylindrical-shaped piece of metal and handed it to his maker.

"Thank you," Timothy said as he unlocked the door. There was a faint clicking sound from inside, and he pulled the door open. "After you," he said to Sheridan, pocketing the key.

They went into the foyer of the house, and Timothy closed the door behind him. As he suspected, the ripple that had gone through the matrix had caused a good many things to be jumbled about. It was obvious that the Wurm had done their best to pick up, but a number of sculptures his father had collected had fallen from their shelf. The Wurm had returned the rubble to the shelf, obviously unsure what to do with it. Timothy supposed he ought to be glad there wasn't more substantial damage.

"It's good to be home," Edgar squawked, spreading his wings and taking flight from Timothy's shoulder. The rook soared around the sprawling foyer, disappearing up the circular staircase to the second floor.

"It is, isn't it," Timothy whispered.

His eyes went to the inventions that he had created after leaving Patience, creations that allowed him to be able to live in the great old house without the gift of magic. The special lamps of hungry fire burned in their places about the lobby. The Wurm had obviously been refilling the oil lamps for him. His eyes traced the piping that ran along the ceiling to bring water by nonmagical means to certain areas of the house. A few of the pipe joints looked as though they might have been damp from leakage. Immediately his mind filled with ideas about how to repair the system and improve it at the same time.

"The house *is* rather dusty, though," Sheridan said, clumping to the stairs before them, and running his segmented metal hand along the railing. He examined the ends of his fingers. He made a clucking noise and a sigh of steam came from the pressure valve on his head. "I can see I'll be busy."

Timothy didn't bother to stop his mechanical friend as he marched off to find a rag. He knew that there were far more important things to worry about than a little dust, but at that moment, he was truly enjoying the warmth of the house, and the memories that flooded his thoughts. He hadn't been living here long before he was whisked off to SkyHaven, but even in that short amount of time, he had developed a connection. This was his father's house, after all, and though he had no magic himself, he could feel the man's presence in every corner. His father's spirit had long since departed, but in some ways, it was in every inch of this house.

Edgar cawed loudly and shouted for Timothy to look out. The boy looked up to see the rook swooping toward him from the second floor. Timothy felt panic race through him, thinking they were under attack, but then he spotted the two Wurm children flying after Edgar. They were smaller than the adults of their kind, but were still quite fearsome to behold.

"I think they want to eat me!" Edgar screeched, landing atop Timothy's head, scratching the boy's scalp as he tried to find purchase, wings fluttering in panic.

The boy reached up and steadied the bird and started to tell Edgar he was being ridiculous, but the two young Wurm flew closer and closer still, and Timothy began to worry. Abruptly they veered off in opposite directions, wings beating the air inside the house, raising dust, until at last they both landed on the foyer floor.

"Greetings, Timothy," one of them said.

"And to all those who call you friend," added the other.

Edgar leaned down from atop Timothy's head to whisper in his ear. "I thought I was a goner," he said breathlessly.

"Hello," Timothy replied, watching as the Wurm landed, their leathery wings furling tightly against their backs. But still he heard the heavy sounds of wings flapping, and looked up again to see the much larger shapes of three adult Wurm as they, too, descended from the upper levels of the house.

One of them was Cythra, the wife of Verlis. Two warriors flanked her. They landed gently at the foot of the stairs, and all bowed their horned heads in greeting.

"It has been too long since last we saw you, Timothy," Cythra growled, her large, yellow eyes mesmerizing in their intensity—and not for the first time, he was quite glad that these fearsome creatures were indeed his friends.

The Wurm of Verlis's clan had been living at the Cade estate since their escape from Draconae a little over a month ago, much to the chagrin of the Parliament of Mages. But these Wurm shared a common foe with the mage guilds, and Timothy hoped that an alliance could be forged between the two.

"Greetings to you, Cythra," Timothy said politely. "I hope that you've been comfortable in my home."

Smoke streamed from her flared nostrils. "Your hospitality to my clan will always be remembered. As your father was accepted into our ranks, so too, do we embrace you as one of our own."

"Hey, imagine that," Edgar croaked. "You're a Wurm now."

Timothy smiled at the thought, proud of the honor, but his smile quickly faded as he recalled the disturbing reason he had returned to his home.

"Something troubles you, Timothy?" Cythra asked, tilting her head to one side. "I presume it involves the anomaly we felt in the matrix of magic. We did our best to restore the house, but some things—"

"That's the least of our concerns, I'm sorry to say," he told her. Timothy took a deep breath before continuing. "Alhazred's Divide has fallen, and Raptus and his followers have come across."

Cythra grunted as if she had been struck, and jets of flame shot from her nostrils. She turned to her warrior companions, and they began to communicate in the strange language of noises that they shared, the snapping of jaws and clicking of tongues. Cythra gestured with a taloned hand to the two younger Wurm, and they immediately took flight, soaring above their heads and up the stairs to the levels above, where the other Wurm were congregated.

She then turned her attention back to Timothy.

"We have anticipated this news," she said in a rumbling growl, "and are ready to assist you in any way that we can."

"I mean you and your clan no disrespect, and I appreciate your offer," he told her. "But I have not yet received word from Parliament that your offer to aid us in our coming struggle has been accepted and—"

"But *we* have," Cythra interrupted.

Timothy frowned in confusion and would have asked her to elaborate, but there came a heavy pounding on the front door.

"Who?" Timothy asked, looking toward the door.

"Maybe Caiaphas has to use the bathroom," Edgar suggested.

The rook fluttered up from his perch on Timothy's shoulder as the boy approached the door. Again there came the heavy knocking, and he slid back the bar and swung open the door, eyes going wide at the sight of the gigantic Lord Romulus standing framed in the doorway.

"Ah, Cade," he said in a rumbling voice, eyes twinkling menacingly from inside the darkness of his horned helmet. "I believe I am expected."

Cassandra strode along a high-ceilinged corridor in Sky-Haven, barely noticing the elegant tapestries that hung from the walls. The sun shone through skylights of spell-glass high above, and she was grateful for the way the warm glow of the day took away some of her exhaustion and anxiety. Sunlight had always had that effect on her.

"Are you sure this is wise?" Carlyle asked, trying to match Cassandra's stride. She was flanked on one side by the fussy little man—she still was having trouble picturing him as a combat mage—and on the other by Ivar, who was having no difficulty keeping up with her.

"Quite sure," Cassandra told him, hearing an edge of authority in her voice that sounded foreign to her. "If we kept Grimshaw here, we could be sure that none of those in Parliament who sympathize with him would come to his rescue, but that is not the law. As Grandmaster, I have no choice but to turn the prisoner over to the proper authorities. What's more, Grimshaw is a danger to the residents of SkyHaven, as well as an unneeded distraction. Moving him to a more secure holding cell at the Xerxis will allow me to concentrate more fully on my duties."

Cassandra picked up her pace, marching down the corridor that would take them outside through a high, arched door and into the courtyard, where the prison transport would be waiting. She wanted to be there to see Grimshaw taken away. As they hurried along, Carlyle became strangely silent, almost reticent. It was not like him at all, and Cassandra shot him a curious sidelong glance.

"What is it?" she asked. "It's not like you to hold your tongue."

"I'm just concerned, Grandmaster. Grimshaw was Alhazred's disciple, and there are bound to be others. We have no way of knowing who they are, or what they might try next."

"Which is exactly why it behooves us to remove him from SkyHaven," she said. "The sooner he is placed inside an inhibitor cell at the Xerxis, the better off we will all be."

With a tiny smile she glanced at Ivar. "How am I doing?"

Even in a hurry, Ivar moved with unequaled grace. He gave her a small nod. "Leander would have been quite proud."

Pride and grief mixed in her heart. Ivar's confidence in her gave her hope, but she mourned the loss of Leander both as her friend, and for the leadership he could have provided during this crisis. It made her all the more determined to be a strong grandmaster for the order.

As they reached the door, Carlyle and Ivar fell behind, and Cassandra waved her hand across the magical eye embedded in the wooden frame. The door swung wide to allow them to exit.

There was a sharp bite to the wind as they went out into the courtyard, a hint of the approaching fall blowing in off the ocean. It whipped Cassandra's red hair around her face, momentarily blinding her. She pushed her hair away and saw that the prisoner transport had already arrived, two uniformed Arcanum law officers flanking the metal vehicle. There was nothing attractive about this means of conveyance. The transport was cold in appearance, made from sharply angled, unadorned metals.

"Here he comes now," Carlyle said, his robes flapping around him as the wind picked up.

Ivar leaned his head back and closed his eyes, seeming to enjoy the wind on his face. Cassandra noticed that his nostrils flared, and suspected that the Asura was sampling the many scents found in the air. *To be so in tune with one's senses,* she thought. *It must be an amazing gift.*

Grimshaw made not a sound as he was brought through a heavy metal door that led down into the dungeons of SkyHaven. The constable was missing an arm—Verlis had bitten it off to keep the fiend from murdering Timothy— so he could not be placed in manacles. There were shackles around his legs, however. They had cleared the courtyard while the transport was there, unwilling to take the chance of innocents being hurt if something should go wrong.

Ivar opened his eyes and glared darkly at Grimshaw. Though he was escorted by six SkyHaven mages, the Asura watched the villain as if he expected Grimshaw to attack them. The thought gave Cassandra a chill, and she was glad to know that Grimshaw wouldn't be kept at the Xerxis indefinitely. As soon as his trial was over, he would wind up in the undersea prison of Abaddon. She shuddered, remembering the stories that Timothy had told her about the place. But if anyone deserved such a horrible fate, it was Grimshaw.

A pulsing ball of white magical energy hovered several feet above the prisoner's head, sapping Grimshaw of his ability to cast spells and wield magic. But as the security team reached the transport with their prisoner, Cassandra heard Ivar utter a sudden gasp. She glanced at him and saw that the black patterns on his bare flesh had begun to darken, moving ominously across the surface of his body.

"Ivar. What's wrong?"

"Something is not right," the Asura said, nostrils twitching. "I can smell it in the air."

Carlyle laughed nervously. "What in the name of the Seven Guardians are you talking about? You cannot *smell* trouble."

Ivar did not respond. He only stared at the transport—more specifically at the two uniformed officers awaiting the transfer.

"The guards," he said, pointing one of his long fingers at the two. "They have the stink of dark magic upon them, and their sweat smells of fear."

The SkyHaven mages escorting Grimshaw had just reached the transport and were exchanging cordial greetings with the transport guards.

"Hold!" Cassandra called, starting toward them. "Wait just a moment, Troy," she said to the senior member of her security team.

All of them glanced her way, and the transport guards must have seen suspicion in her eyes, for in that instant they revealed their betrayal. Before Cassandra could shout a warning, they were in motion, magic crackling around their clenched fists. Spells burst from their hands, slamming into the SkyHaven security mages and throwing them back, away from Grimshaw.

They turned and thrust their hands out, blue-black magic churning around their fingers before it lanced outward, directly at Cassandra. Carlyle grabbed her around the waist and dropped to the ground, pulling her after him. The murderous magic burned the air above their heads as it passed by.

"Curse them! This is precisely what I was afraid of!" Carlyle snarled.

None of the security mages were moving, and Cassandra hoped they were only unconscious. The transport guards focused their magical attack on the inhibitor spell hovering over Grimshaw's head, dispersing it with a conjoined blast of disruptive power. Cassandra watched in horror, realizing that Carlyle had been correct indeed, and that if Grimshaw escaped, it would be her responsibility, her first act as true Grandmaster of the order. She would not have it.

"Stop them! He's going to escape," Cassandra cried, leaping to her feet and conjuring a spell that would shatter the betrayers' bones and the transport alike.

"Mistress, no!" Carlyle shouted.

The traitors were too fast, unleashing crackling bolts of magic that threw up a defensive shield, deflecting her attack, the magic dispersing in the air. A triumphant shout drew her attention, and she looked over to see Grimshaw laughing, magic swelling around him as though he could barely contain it. It was purplish black, the color of a bruise. But far worse was the fact that Grimshaw's missing arm had been replaced by a strange, multi-tentacled appendage seemingly composed of pure dark magic.

As she and Carlyle watched in shock and revulsion, Grimshaw's roiling black tentacles entwined his would-be rescuers.

"You can assist me in one final way," she heard the former constable bellow. "I have need of your life energies."

The transport guards screamed as their flesh withered and their life force was drained away. Their empty uniforms fluttered to the ground, and their ashes were whisked away on the wind.

"Grimshaw!" Cassandra shouted as she stumbled toward the dark mage.

Carlyle was beside her. His hands glowed with a bright golden light as he summoned an assault of combat magic. Cassandra did the same, spreading her legs in a battle stance as she mustered all her strength into a single attack spell. As one, they shouted and unleashed their magic.

That disgusting, serpentine limb spread into a black, oily cloud of magic, and the spells they had cast disappeared inside. Grimshaw only laughed.

"Nothing would make me happier than to stay and chat with you, my dear," he snarled. "But I have places to go. People to meet."

The magical arm suddenly whipped out as if with a mind of its own, and struck the young Grandmaster in the center of the chest with a crackling snap. Cassandra was hurled violently backward by the force of the assault. She rolled across the ground, certain that she would have been dead if she hadn't managed to erect a shield of defense mere moments before the dark magic touched her. When she crawled to her knees, she saw that Carlyle was down as well. Down and not moving.

Grimshaw was already climbing into the transport. "Alliances must be made," she heard him say as the door swung shut behind him. Then there came the roar of the prison transport's magically fueled engines, and the vehicle rose up, escaping SkyHaven with no further resistance.

Cassandra rushed to her assistant. "Carlyle! Are you all right?"

He groaned as he opened his eyes, and then a scowl twisted his face. "Grimshaw!" Carlyle shouted as he pushed himself up. "We can't let him—"

"Too late, I'm afraid." Cassandra shook her head. She looked around the courtyard at the security mages, who were at last rising from the ground, holding their heads and wincing with pain. "I've really made a mess of things."

Carlyle sighed. "No. No, you haven't, mistress. Only the traitors who aided Grimshaw were killed. Otherwise, no one was badly hurt. You took all the necessary precautions. What else could we have done?"

She stared at him. "We could have stopped him. You

don't have to be so gentle with me, Carlyle. I am the Grandmaster now. You shared your fears and I dismissed them. I was a fool."

Carlyle rose to his feet and looked around. At last he met her gaze. "We'll get him, Grandmaster. Eventually we will find him again. Mark my words."

"Indeed," she replied, still feeling like a complete fool. "Notify the authorities at once to give chase. It cannot be too difficult to track a stolen prison transport."

"I'm not sure about that," Carlyle said.

"And why not?"

"Grimshaw is traveling south," Carlyle explained. "Heading toward—"

"Tora'nah and the invaders from Draconae," Cassandra finished, cold fingers of dread brushing against the nape of her neck. Now she understood the last words Grimshaw had spoken.

Alliances must be made.

"He's going to Raptus," Cassandra said quietly. "Grimshaw is going to ally himself with Raptus. We have to warn Timothy."

She looked around for Ivar, to ask him to hurry to August Hill with the terrible news, but he was nowhere to be found. Cassandra called his name, scanning the courtyard, new fear growing in her heart.

"I saw him moving toward the transport just after you were struck down," Carlyle said. "You don't think he might have . . ."

The question hung unanswered in the air, as Cassandra gazed off in the direction the craft had flown.

"He might have," she answered in a fearful whisper, the whereabouts of the Asura now weighing heavily upon her.

CHAPTER FOUR

General Raptus watched with uneasy fascination as the device that the mages called the Burrower dug through the first layers of dirt and rock, and he was glad that he had ordered his raiders to keep some of the mages alive. Mercy had not caused him to do this. It was practicality. It had been ages since the Wurm roamed free in this world, and to learn what he could of its current events—its most vulnerable targets and most important leaders—he would have to interrogate prisoners.

Now, though, he had found another use for those he had allowed to live: operating the Burrower. The mages had seemed horrified when he instructed them to dig up the tombs of the Dragons of Old, the ancient burial ground of his own kind. The weakling Verlis had instructed them never to defile that land. But Raptus had set them to digging immediately.

He was searching for something.

His soldiers could have used their talons to dig down into the rock and soil, but the mages had found a way to accomplish his chore all the faster. Raptus also enjoyed the irony that if he did find the object of his search, the mages' inventiveness would have helped to hasten their own extermination.

The Burrower bucked, rocked, and whined as its spinning nose tore into the sacred ground. Raptus looked from the deepening hole to the mage who operated the digging mechanism. The man's face was flushed and pink, his eyes bulging in their sockets. It was obvious that he was terrified of failing at the task Raptus had assigned him. Yasgul, one of general's more sadistic soldiers, sat crouched behind the man with sword in hand, adding to the pathetic mage's terror. *It was how all humans should behave in the presence of their superiors,* Raptus thought. And soon he would make that belief a reality.

"Is this wise?" asked a raspy voice.

Raptus whipped around, twin gouts of flame leaping out from his flared nostrils. He looked upon the grim and scarred face of Hannuk, one of his most trusted advisors.

"You question me, Hannuk?"

"I mean you no disrespect, General." Hannuk averted his eyes. "But why do you tempt the spirits of our ancient ancestors by defiling their final resting place with that"—he gestured with his hand toward the digging machine—"that damnable thing."

Raptus looked back to the Burrower, its cylindrical body penetrating the ground farther, toppling the long-standing stones that marked the graves of the species that had evolved into the Wurm. It was a sad sight indeed, but necessary if the future that he imagined for his people was ever to come to pass.

"It is a sacrifice that must be made," Raptus snarled, watching as the device continued its progress, digging deeper and deeper into the cold, hard ground of Tora'nah. "The mages have provided us with a way to hasten our plans. I have no compunction about using their invention to acquire what is needed to achieve this victory."

"What *is* needed?" Hannuk asked, moving nearer. "We have breached the divide and our forces are resolute and strong." He blew a stream of orange fire into the air. "Now we lay siege to the Xerxis, and the accursed Parliament of Mages, and make those responsible for their treachery pay dearly."

It's all so simple for him, Raptus thought. Hannuk believed so strongly in their superiority, but his faith was unfounded. The mages of Terra drastically outnumbered the Wurm— thousands to one—and their combat mages wielded sorcery vastly more powerful than what the Wurm had at their disposal.

A horrible shriek like the birth cries of a thousand hatchlings filled the cold air of Tora'nah, and Raptus spun to see that the Burrower had struck something. Green, foul-smelling gas erupted like a geyser from the massive hole in the ground.

Both the mage operating the machine and Yasgul, his guard, began to choke, coughing uncontrollably as the noxious fumes assailed them. Raptus strode toward the excavation, Hannuk at his side. Cautiously they approached the ragged edge. The air was befouled by the escaping gas, and they both unfurled their wings to fan it away.

"You talk of destroying the mages," Raptus said as he peered into the thick, roiling green cloud. "But their numbers are far superior to ours, and their magic is great. Without some other advantage, we have no hope against them."

The general gestured for the Burrower to be retracted from the hole, and the digging machine slowly began to withdraw, moving backward up the ramp with the whirring and grinding of its mechanical innards.

"No mage can stand before us," Hannuk argued as Raptus leaped down into the gaping hole. "We have the furnace of hatred in our hearts, our fire consumes them, and we come as death from above—"

"The mages would strike us all down in a matter of days," Raptus said with a growl as he landed atop the flat piece of gray stone that had been cracked by the spinning head of the Burrower. "First they would be afraid, but then they would gather their numbers, pooling their magical might to see us dead."

Raptus knelt, his wings continuing to fan away the thick, greenish fog that leaked from the jagged crack in the stone beneath his taloned feet.

"Then what are we going to do?" Hannuk asked, peering over the edge of the hole. "Do we stay here, waiting for the arrival of the mages—for our inevitable deaths? You promised vengeance upon our betrayers, Raptus. How will this ever come to pass if we do not attack?"

The general worked his claws into a crack in the stone and then tore it up and away. "I did not say we would not attack."

"But how will we—"

"As a hatchling the ancient beliefs were taught to me by a wizened Wurm called Barrakus," the general explained. "In me he saw something special, and because of that he shared a secret that had been kept by members of his clan for countless ages—a secret meant only to be revealed to the one who could potentially change the destiny of the Wurm."

Raptus reached down into the darkness of the breach he had just torn in the slab of rock, his hands falling upon the warm, smooth surface of an object that his people had believed only legend.

"Barrakus believed me to be that Wurm, Hannuk," Raptus said, and slowly he withdrew his hands from the darkness, holding an enormous egg-shaped thing of the same sickly green as the gas that had come from that hole.

"And with this, I intend to prove him right."

While he had been imprisoned in a dungeon cell in Sky-Haven, his ability to cast magic taken from him by an inhibitor sphere, Arturo Grimshaw had come to the most horrific of realizations.

He needed to become what he most despised.

Now the former constable piloted the prison transport south, his arm, composed entirely of magic, manipulating the controls of the sky craft with ease, bending the spells that powered the airship to his will. The transport soared above the rich, dark green of the Yarrith Forest, and onward toward Tora'nah, and his new destiny as a creature of chaos.

His entire life had been about the pursuit of order, and he was certain that this was why his master, Alhazred, had originally sought him out as a boy. The archmage saw in him the ability to do great things, to bend chaos to his will, and to bring about control. And that was exactly what he had done, first as a security officer and then by quickly moving up the ranks to become constable. The secret power of Alhazred had fueled his ambitions, and he had served the archmage well, but now his dark master was dead, and he felt his tenuous grasp on the order of his world slipping through his fingers.

He had first felt this upon learning of the Cade boy—the un-magician—but had faith in his own abilities, and his dark master's growing might. The freak of a boy would be only a minor irritant, dealt with swiftly.

If only that had been the case.

Grimshaw felt his entire body begin to tremble at the thought of the boy. *How is it possible that this one child has been responsible for effecting so much change in the world? It's almost as if young Cade is somehow the personification of chaos.* A chill ran through him at the thought.

He was unsure how much farther he had to travel, and conjured a map that floated in the air so that he could check his progress. His means of transport appeared as a bright red dot on the magical map, and Tora'nah as a star of yellow. *It won't be long now,* he mused, estimating the distance in hours. Plenty of time to adjust his way of thinking to reflect the pandemonium that had infected the world.

Alhazred was dead, and the Wurm had invaded. If there were any clear signs that chaos had taken control, this was the most obvious. Sitting within his cold, dark cell, stripped of all that defined him, Grimshaw had realized that he had to change in order to live. A pure creature of order could not survive a world in constant flux. No, he needed to become what he most hated.

A creature of disorder, an enemy of harmony.

A beast of chaos.

And he could think of no one better to help him with his transformation than the leader of the Wurm invaders. He had much to share with the monsters. And if everything went according to plan, Raptus would have much to share with him.

For the first time in his life, Ivar wished that he were riding *inside* a sky craft. He hated the unnatural feeling of confinement they gave him. But that confinement would have been preferable to his current situation.

The Asura clung to the back of the prison transport, using all his focus to keep his grip firm. If he was not careful, the strong winds that buffeted him as the stolen transport flew south would tear him from his perch. As his fingers began to cramp and grow numb with the cold, Ivar was forced to wonder if he had made a fatal mistake.

Yet there had been no choice. Grimshaw had been escaping, and Ivar could not bear the thought of a villain such as he going free. Blending with the surroundings so as not to be seen, Ivar had leaped onto the back of the ascending prison transport. Though not as sophisticated as the laws set down by the mages, the Asura had their own system of justice that had served them well in their day. It was elegantly simple. If one did wrong, than one was punished by a member of the tribe who had been designated as *Lawgiver*—the keeper of tribal law and order.

As the last of his kind, he had no choice but to designate himself as Lawgiver, and swore, as he clung to back of the prison transport, that Grimshaw would not be allowed to hurt any of his friends—the tribe he had surrounded himself with—or perform any act of evil again.

So said Ivar, last of the Asura.

So said the Lawgiver.

Cythra perched at the edge of the rooftop, stretching her leathery wings to their full span as she looked out over August Hill and at the sprawling metropolis of Arcanum below. It was obvious to Timothy that she was more comfortable here, less cramped.

"He'll want to see that in ruin," she said, pointing a black claw at the spires of Arcanum twinkling in the distance.

Her clan soared in the sky above, dipping and weaving and blowing fire at one another as they trained for the coming battle. They were a fearsome sight to behold, but a small voice in the back of Timothy's mind continued to ask the question *Will it be enough?*

Lord Romulus paced nervously about the rooftop, not at all comfortable in the presence of the female Wurm.

"The foul beast will never be allowed to reach Arcanum," he blustered, clasping his gauntleted hands behind his back and sticking out his broad, armored chest. "Our security forces are more than enough to repel any such attack. The Legion Nocturne alone will stop him. Raptus's filth will never come north of my fortress at Twilight."

Something nagged at Timothy, an irritant of a question that refused to be quelled no matter how hard he tried. He could no longer hold his tongue.

"Raptus isn't stupid," he blurted out.

Cythra turned her large, horned head to look at him. Romulus glowered.

"I was his captive for a while. This isn't some reckless troublemaker without a plan."

"We are well aware of the danger posed by our enemy, boy," Romulus said, his eyes blazing from black pools inside his helmet. The mage was a giant by any standard, at least ten feet tall, and the nearer Timothy got to him, the more intimidating Romulus was. He reached up to stroke the long hair of his beard. "It matters not at all. Our forces are superior. Even if our power and valor were not enough, our numbers would crush him."

It was Timothy's turn to pace. Something continued to nag at him.

"And that's what I can't understand."

"Explain yourself, Timothy," Cythra asked, folding her wings against her back, eyes narrow with worry.

"He would know that he couldn't win," the boy said. "How many soldiers does he have? Two hundred? Maybe three hundred if you count the laborers from Draconae, plus a handful of Wurm sorcerers. He'll either have left the families back in Draconae or resettled them in Tora'nah, but he won't have them fighting. The children and the aged, young mothers—they won't be part of the attack against us. So let us say three hundred. What chance would they have against a city of hundreds of thousands of mages? Not to mention the other settlements they will have to conquer just to get to Arcanum. It just doesn't make sense."

The sound of Romulus chuckling filled the air like the growl of a hungry predator. "Isn't it obvious to you both?" he asked them. "Raptus is mad. His hate for the mages of Terra has made him irrational. It would not be the first time that a tyrant infected with the disease of insanity has waged an impossible war against a much larger and more powerful foe."

"The boy is right," Cythra said in a hushed whisper, twin streams of hissing steam flowing up from her nostrils. "I have known Raptus since he was a hatchling—we grew up together—were even friends in the early days of our youth. He has never been a fool."

Romulus moved closer to them. "What are the two of you suggesting?" he asked, caution in his low, grumbling tone.

Timothy sighed, not caring for the direction his thoughts were taking him. "It's just that I can't imagine that he would invade Terra without some kind of plan. Some way that would guarantee a victory."

And as those words left his lips, he heard a sharp intake of air from Cythra that could only have been a gasp of shock.

"What is it, Cythra?" he asked, imagining that he saw a look of fear in the dark, watery eyes of Verlis's mate. "What did I say?"

"All this talk of Raptus has stirred the flames of remembrance," she said. "Even as a youth, his hate for the mages knew no bounds. His nature was scarred by the death of his father before his hatching."

Romulus crossed his arms and grumbled in frustration. "What has this to do with now?"

Cythra ignored the petulant attitude of the leader of the Legion Nocturne, lost in memories of days gone by. "Even as a child his thoughts did not stray from the idea of revenge, and how he would eventually achieve it. But Raptus was also obsessed with the legends of the Dragons of Old. There was one particular legend that he often talked about. It was said that the dragons feared the growing power of the wizards with whom they shared this world. The dragons feared that there would come a day when their kind would be no more."

Romulus threw his hand up in frustration, bellowing at the heavens. "We have no time for myths and legends! Our enemy moves against us!"

Timothy cast an angry eye toward the Grandmaster. "Please, Lord Romulus, be patient," the boy snapped. "Go on, Cythra. We're listening."

"With their ancient sorcery, legend claims that the dragons created a horrible weapon, an egg."

Timothy frowned. "They created an egg . . . as a weapon? I don't—"

"Not just any egg," Cythra explained, leaning in closer to make sure he understood the importance of what it was she was saying. "They called it the Spawn of Wrath, and inside its shell seethed the fury, rage, and fear of all dragonkind. A power that, if consumed, could bestow upon the eater unspeakable might."

The Wurm pulled her wings tightly around her, as if suddenly cold. "Raptus often spoke of one day having his vengeance. There were other ideas he had to achieve that end, but he returned to the tale of the Spawn of Wrath more than any other. I paid no mind to his rambling, for it was only a legend, after all."

"Precisely!" Romulus snarled. "It is a thing of legend— of myth. It doesn't exist."

Timothy felt a chill pass through him, and he gnawed his lower lip. "But what if it does?"

Cythra shrugged her broad shoulders. "It was said that the Spawn was buried with the Queen, hidden with her body in the final resting place of the dragons."

"Tora'nah," Timothy whispered, a claw of fear gripping at his chest.

The Wurm nodded. "If it does exist, that is where it would be found."

"And if he does find it?" Romulus asked. "What then? What can we do to defend ourselves?"

Cythra did not answer, turning her gaze up to the members of her tribe that flew above their heads. She spread her wings, leaping up into the sky to join them in flight.

Her silence spoke volumes.

CHAPTER FIVE

A cold rain had started to fall over the burial ground, almost as if the Dragons of Old were crying tears of joy over what he had found. Raptus could not pull his gaze from his prize—from the Spawn of Wrath. It was exactly as he believed, not only a thing of legend, but of the physical world. It existed—in all its wondrous glory. And now, it belonged to him.

Through the shell of the great egg he felt the thrum of ancient power, waiting to be unleashed.

"Do you see it, Hannuk?" Raptus asked. "In my hands, I hold the future."

The old Wurm recoiled as the general held the egg out to him, almost as if he could sense the power roiling inside the fragile shell, and was terrified by it.

"How is this possible?" Hannuk asked, his rough voice

now an awe-filled whisper. "In all my years I never would have believed that it could be true."

Raptus held the Spawn of Wrath all the higher, showing it to all his soldiers, who had gathered at his request.

"Look upon its magnificence and believe!" he bellowed. The rain began to fall harder, and he was certain that many present didn't understand the full ramifications of the prize. The legends of the ancients were practically forgotten by the younger generations of Wurm, but he would teach them— show them the extent of its ancient might.

The survivors of the mining operation had been gathered as well, corralled together, their heads bowed in a pathetic mixture of defeat and fear. Raptus moved toward them, his prize held out before him. He wanted them to see the object of their eventual destruction.

"Do you see, mages?" he asked as he held the Spawn out to them. Most raised their heads, eyes fixing on the egg. Steam rose from its smooth, yellow surface as the rain landed on it. "This was created because of you—because of the fear and the disloyalty you inspire, and the misery and pain you bring. You have done this."

They stood silently, their faces covered in dirt, ash, and blood. Yet there was a low rustle of voices in the air. At first he thought the whispering came from somewhere behind him, and he whirled around to listen. But then Raptus realized that the voices were coming from the egg—the Spawn was speaking to him.

And Raptus listened.

The collected rage and fear of his ancestors spoke to him, thousands upon thousands of ghostly voices clamoring to fill his skull. The egg started to vibrate, a pulsing glow beginning to emanate from within. And the dead continued to chatter and wail, every detail of the indignities suffered by the ancient species at the hands of the mages pouring into his head.

His own rage was fed by the rabid emotions of the ancients, and he thought he would explode. Raptus began to tremble and the egg to vibrate. It seemed to be growing larger in his hands, and he almost cried out, but he found that his tongue was paralyzed and his eyes were locked on the yellowed surface of the Spawn of Wrath.

It was almost too much for him to bear, and he attempted to release the egg, to let it drop—and likely shatter upon the sacred ground of Tora'nah—but it would not let him. It was as if his hands had become part of the Spawn's surface, and no matter how hard he tried, he could not be free of it. Raw, razor-sharp emotions flowed through his body like the most powerful of magical spells, and he was assaulted on every sensory level, driven nearly to the brink of madness.

Raptus was certain that he was about to die, that the frenzied emotions of the Dragons of Old were so starved for revenge that their eagerness would snuff out his life. He could sense his soldiers watching him, not sure what they should do. He wanted to cry out for any of them to relieve him of this horrific burden. But the dragons would not allow it. There was so much they had to tell him.

It was too much to bear, and it drove him to his knees. Still he held on to his prize—a prize that had unexpectedly become a curse. He felt his sense of self slowly slipping away. All that remained was a primitive, snarling beast, an animal that would do anything to survive.

Raptus tossed back his head, roaring up into the storm-filled skies, before bringing his mouth down, biting into the shell of the Spawn of Wrath. He felt the surface of the Spawn crack, heard the shrieks and wails of the ghostly voices trapped within cry out all the louder, as if excited by his attack. Again and again the tyrant bit down upon the hard surface of the Spawn, as more and more fractures appeared in its yellowed shell.

Then he snapped his jaws closed in a final, tremendous bite, an attack that would have snapped bone and torn sinew. The shell shattered, exposing the roiling contents of the Spawn of Wrath, bathing Raptus in the collected hatred of a race long gone. It enveloped him, crawling inside the warmth of his body to make itself at home.

Raptus shrieked a cry of the damned as magical energies merged with his body, flowing out from his talons to strike at the burial ground on which he stood. And as the magic of the ancient dragons touched it, the ground began to bubble and froth as though it were liquid.

He spread his wings and took to the sky, feeling the presence of the dragons in every aspect of his body—filling him up with unbridled fury, making him thirst for the opportunity to reap his revenge—*their* revenge at last.

Everything is different now, he thought as he soared above the human excavation at Tora'nah. Before, he would dream of possessing a power that would allow him to see his enemies vanquished, and now that had been realized and the power belonged to him.

Raptus came to a halt above the gathered mages, his powerful wings pounding the air with mighty beats to keep himself aloft. He stared down at them, studying each and every one. He wanted to remember them, the first to fall before the unbridled fury joined to his own.

"You are but the first," he roared, the bubbling of liquid fire percolating in his chest before his mouth opened, and the flames, fueled by his own wrath and the wrath of dead dragons, came forth to reduce the human prisoners to ash.

Raptus then dropped from the sky to kneel among the still-smoldering remains of his vanquished enemy. He furled his wings, hearing the sound of someone approaching behind him.

"General Raptus," Hannuk said with caution. "Are you . . . are you well?"

And Raptus turned to look upon his second in command with new eyes.

A conqueror's eyes.

"Hannuk, dear friend," he growled, fresh fire bubbling in his throat. "I've never been better."

The two young Wurm were chasing him again.

Edgar flew swiftly down the long, first-floor corridor,

looking for someplace to hide from the mischievous youngsters. He knew that they were only playing, but their playing often had a tendency to get a little rough, and he had the singed tail feathers to show for it.

Ahead he could see that the door to Argus Cade's study hung partway open, and he breathed a sigh of relief, flapping his wings all the harder for that extra burst of speed to get to his oasis of safety more quickly. Angling his body in such a way as to fit, the rook soared through the opening, stomach and back feathers gently brushing against the door and frame.

"Better lay off the sweets," he grumbled.

Edgar fluttered around the study and went back to the door. Touching down in front of the opening, he could hear the sound of the young Wurm's approach. He placed his side against the wood and gave it a push. The door shut, and the black bird breathed a sigh of relief. He heard their playful laughter as they went past the door, wondering aloud where he had hidden. In moments the sounds receded. They would eventually tire of searching for him or something else would distract them. Wurm children had very short attention spans.

Left alone in the study, Edgar spread his wings and launched himself upward to land atop the desk that had once belonged to his master, Argus Cade. It was strange to see it uncluttered. When Argus was alive, it had always been laden with scrolls and mystical artifacts. As the familiar to Argus Cade—companion, servant, messenger, and confidant—Edgar had felt privileged to know a mage with such honor and such brilliance. Now he had the pleasure of serving his former master's son.

Most familiars passed on with the death of their masters, but something had kept Edgar in the world. Perhaps Argus had arranged for it, or perhaps it was simply his purpose.

The bird hopped about the desktop, remembering earlier times. He missed Argus Cade terribly. It was the first time since the archmage's death that he had actually had the opportunity to reminisce about his old friend. He wondered what Argus would have thought of how much things had changed since Timothy stepped out of Patience: the fall of Nicodemus, the coming of Verlis and his tribe, the revelation that Alhazred was still alive, and now the Wurm invasion.

Edgar shivered, ruffling his feathers. It was enough to make a sane bird go entirely mad. It had been one crisis after another, and the rook wondered what new obstacle could possibly be waiting over the next horizon.

As if on cue, he smelled something in the air: a peculiar scent, sharp, yet oddly sweet. It was an odor that Edgar had not experienced since . . .

In a corner of the study bordered by bookcases, the air began to distort, to shimmer and quake as something began to manifest.

"Here we go again," the rook whispered, transfixed to the sight of the dimensional doorway opening in the study of Argus Cade, providing some unknown intruder passage from someplace else—to here.

Edgar braced as the vortex of magic opened in the air, a blast of cold air and snow from the other side of the rift nearly knocking him from his perch atop the desk. Lifting a wing, he shielded his eyes from the blowing ice and snow, attempting to discern the shapes that were exiting from the magical rip torn in time and space.

Carefully he hopped toward the edge of the desk, closer to the study door. If necessary, he could make a quick dash to the door, get it open, and warn Timothy and the others that they were in danger. If necessary, but something told the bird it wouldn't be the case.

They emerged from the dimensional portal, trembling figures clad in snow-covered armor, spilling into the warmth of the deceased mage's study. Edgar's suspicions as to who they were, and how they came to be in Argus Cade's study, were confirmed as the last of the armored figures stumbled from the portal floating in the air, followed by the large, bestial shape of Verlis.

Edgar experienced a wave of relief upon seeing his friend. They'd had no idea what had happened to him when Alhazred's Divide had fallen, and Raptus and his army had entered the world. It was good to see that he was safe, and that other members of the Tora'nah expedition had made it out safely as well. There were eight so far, and Edgar craned his neck from his perch to see if any more would follow Verlis into the room.

But there didn't seem to be any others.

The Wurm turned toward the whirlpool of magic, his

fingers moving in the air before it, closing down the entry-way.

The dimensional rip sealed with a thunderous clap, and Edgar took flight from the desk to glide around his friend's head.

"Verlis! Glad to see you in one piece," Edgar croaked. "Your family kept saying they were sure they would have known if you were dead, that you must still be alive, but I don't think Tim believed them."

Verlis looked at him then, his eyes filled with intensity.

"Take me to him," the Wurm said gravely. "Our darkest fears have come true. Bring me to Timothy at once."

It never seems to slow down, Edgar thought as he flew from the study, Verlis and the workers of Tora'nah following behind. *From one thing to the next.*

The life of a familiar. It's exhausting.

They had all crammed into the kitchen.

Timothy busied himself at the stove he had modified using a combination of heatstone and hungry fire as opposed to magic. He was eager to help the blacksmiths, volunteering to heat a large pot of spiced brew to drive the chill from their frozen bones.

Now he turned away from the stove. It would be a moment longer before the water had boiled enough to make the drinks, and he took the time to survey the gathering. The kitchen was large by all standards, but it strained to hold all who were present at the moment.

The blacksmiths and miners sat with Walter Telford around the large kitchen table, blankets taken from the many rooms in the Cade estate draped over their shoulders. Timothy had been glad to see that Walter and the smiths had survived, but very disheartened by the fact that there had not been more. The thought of all the others who had not lived through Raptus's attack filled him with sadness, and he continued to look about the crowded kitchen in an attempt to distract himself.

Lord Romulus stood by the door, arms folded across his barrel chest. Timothy found it amusing that the Grandmaster of the Legion Nocturne had to bend his head ever so slightly so that the horns of his helmet did not scratch the kitchen ceiling.

Verlis and Cythra huddled close in the far corner of the room. It was obvious to Tim that the couple was quite pleased to be in each other's company again. It was one ray of light in these dark times.

Edgar and Sheridan stood vigilantly by his side, as they always did. He could ask for friends no better than these.

The large pot of water over the hungry flame on the stove began to boil, and Timothy turned away from the silent gathering to prepare the spiced beverage. "This should just take a minute," he said, picking up a glass jar of rich-smelling spices and herbs and dumping all the contents into the frothing water.

"Let me assist you with that," Sheridan said, sidling toward him and gently pushing him away. "You have much more important things to concern yourself with."

Timothy started to protest, but knew that his mechanical friend was right. There was no avoiding it any longer. They needed to discuss the approaching war.

"First of all," he began, looking around at the gathering, "let me say how glad I am that you made it back."

Sheridan had begun to disperse the cups of brew, offering the first to Walter Telford. The mage thanked the mechanical man and, shrugging off his blanket, rose to his feet. He held the mug in his hands and gazed around at the seven men and women who had survived the invasion of Tora'nah with him.

"It's good to be alive," he said, his voice choked with emotion as he made eye contact with all of the three miners and four blacksmiths who had fought at his side. "But I propose a toast to those who weren't so lucky," he said as he raised his steaming mug. "And for those who will risk so much in the coming conflict."

The cups of brew had all been handed out and Timothy watched as all those gathered in the room—Wurm and grandmaster alike—lifted their cups in solidarity.

"For all who have sacrificed, and those who will sacrifice, we salute you," Telford said.

In grave silence they drank to the dead and the daring.

"Excuse me," Edgar croaked from a nearby shelf, his head cocked to one side quizzically. "But why does it feel like we've already fought this war and lost?"

Everyone looked startled, glancing about at one another,

and Timothy thanked the bird with the slightest of nods. Edgar's curt admonition was exactly what they all needed.

"The bird is right," Romulus said, setting his cup down. Officially he was here as an ambassador from the Parliament of Mages, but Timothy was pleased to see that he seemed to be growing comfortable in this group. "Yes, these are dire times, but there is still hope—still a battle to be fought."

Verlis exhaled a hissing cloud of steam and shook his head nervously. "But the Spawn of Wrath—if that is indeed what Raptus was searching for—how can we oppose such power?"

Timothy set his cup down on the table. All eyes were suddenly on him. "We oppose it the only way we know how," he said. "By using every resource we have available to us."

He continued to look about the room, at all who had gathered there.

"We fight them with the magic of all the guilds in Parliament, not just combat mages, but every single person who can stand against them. We fight them with Malleum armor forged by Terra's finest blacksmiths," he said, pointing out Walter and his people. He then turned his attention to Verlis and Cythra. "And with the ferocity of your clan."

They were all staring at him now, their eyes sparking with what he imagined to be hope. "We fight them together."

Beneath the medicine-soaked wrappings, Cassandra Nicodemus's delicate fingertips, burned from the excessive use of defensive magic, throbbed uncomfortably. She sat in the back of the traveling sky carriage with Carlyle beside her and looked at her hands. She'd never imagined having to use her magical talents in such a violent fashion, and here she was, striking out with such unbridled fury that she had actually burned the skin of her fingertips. Her combat with the creature her grandfather had become, and then her attempts at halting Grimshaw's escape, flashed through her mind, and it all seemed so wild, so unlike the life she was used to.

"Do they bother you, mistress?" Carlyle asked, and she blinked, having barely heard the question.

"Your fingers," he said, nodding toward her still upraised hands. "Do they pain you?"

Slowly she returned her injured hands to her lap, gazing out the window of the carriage as they flew over the vast city of Arcanum toward Xerxis. "A little, but they'll be fine in time."

"It takes time and strict discipline to learn to wield combat magic on that scale without injury," Carlyle said, glancing casually into his schedule book as he spoke.

"I'm well aware of that, thank you," she answered, annoyed at this discussion of what she thought of as her inadequacies.

"Perhaps, once this is all over, and things have returned to some semblance of order . . . I could teach you," the former combat mage said haltingly, careful in case he should unintentionally insult her.

Instead Cassandra was touched by the offer. Carlyle was

as fussy and self-important a man as she had ever met, but she had recently discovered this other side of him. He cared far too much for rules and propriety, but his history as a combat mage revealed that there was more to him than that. It was kind of him to offer to help her learn.

"I'd like that very much," she said, turning away from the view of the city to meet his gaze. "I'm certain there is a great deal I could learn from you."

Carlyle seemed pleased, but once again he glanced down to check the documents he carried. "It would be helpful, I think. As Grandmaster you will need to master all forms of magic, defensive as well as offensive."

Cassandra might have replied, but in that moment the Xerxis came into view far below, and any response died on her lips. She was always breathless at the majesty of the headquarters of the Parliament, particularly its central spire. The tower was a marvel, formed by four beams that curved halfway up, twisting in upon themselves so that the tower grew narrower and narrower. It was the oldest structure in all of Arcanum, and it never failed to inspire her. Even as a child, looking at pictographs of the ancient city, the home of the Parliament of Mages was always her personal favorite; and here she was, Grandmaster of one of the most powerful magical orders, the Xerxis now part of her day-to-day life— and now temporarily to become her home.

She smiled at the thought despite the heaviness of the mood.

"Carlyle, do you think I made the right decision?"

Her assistant glanced up, brow knitted. "You mean relocating essential personnel from SkyHaven to the Xerxis?"

For a moment her attention was caught by the view out the window. She saw six more sky carriages spread out in the air around their own, all of them carrying Order of Alhazred acolytes and security staff. Then she glanced at Carlyle and nodded.

"I hated the idea of leaving SkyHaven," he said with obvious sincerity. "But with all the troubles we've had there of late—secret chambers, mages long thought dead still alive, the entire structure nearly falling from the sky into the ocean, and Grimshaw's escape to the south—we cannot guarantee that the fortress is secure. Grimshaw could lead Raptus right to SkyHaven." Carlyle nodded. "So yes, I think you've made the correct choice."

"I hope Ivar is all right," she said worriedly, glancing out the carriage window again as the craft began its descent to the landing zone of the Xerxis plaza.

"The Asura is quite formidable. I suspect he can take care of himself."

Cassandra hoped he was right. One of the Parliament guards patrolling the landing zone came over to open her door and she climbed from her transport.

"The Voice is awaiting your arrival with the other members of Parliament, Grandmaster," the guard said with a courteous bow.

"Excellent."

"I've also been instructed to show your staff to their temporary quarters," the man added.

She looked to Carlyle, now standing by her side. "Go along with them, please, and make sure that they're settled. I'll be along whenever the meeting finishes."

"Very good, mistress," Carlyle said, going to meet the rest of the transplanted SkyHaven staff as their sky carriages landed.

Cassandra watched him for a moment, wondering how it had all come to this. The days when simple politics and betrayal among the guilds were the worst things they had to worry about were long behind them. At length she turned and allowed the guard to escort her through the front door of the Xerxis.

Two more sentries awaited her there, a woman and a man, each of them bowing as she passed beneath the large archway into the foyer. They touched two fingers to their foreheads, then to their hearts in salute.

"Grandmaster Nicodemus," they said in unison. "Kind thoughts on this most troubling of days."

"On this and all days," she responded with a short bow.

The female sentry motioned with her arm for Cassandra to pass and she did so, following the long corridor to the large parliamentary chamber at its end. She heard the commotion even before she entered, voices raised in heated discussion.

She entered the vast, circular chamber and caught sight of Alethea Borgia, Grandmaster of the Tantrus Order and reigning Voice of Parliament, standing on the dais in the center. All around her was chaos, the chatter almost deafening.

The room was the heart of the Xerxis, and its walls went all the way up to the apex of the tower itself. The grandmasters of Parliament, raging in argument, played havoc with the room's acoustics.

Cassandra walked down an aisle into the room, approaching the center stage and the Voice.

Alethea turned her eyes from the commotion to take notice of her arrival. The Voice appeared much older somehow than the last time Cassandra had seen her.

"Welcome to Parliament, Grandmaster Nicodemus," the Voice said, gesturing toward the commotion with no small irony.

Cassandra glanced around her at the chaos in the room. She had been to only a few of the parliamentary gatherings, but they had never been like this. "What . . . what's happening?"

The Voice laughed sadly. "This is what we have come to," she said with a shake of her head. "I could control them no longer. Their passions have gotten the better of them, and they no longer seem to remember that they are supposed to be above such behavior, shining examples to the world in which we live. I thought rather than steal their voices away yet again, I ought to let them bluster until they're tired of it themselves."

Cassandra watched as the other grandmasters ranted and raved, and suddenly felt very, very afraid for the world in which she lived. "What has divided them so?"

"Foolishness. Though the danger has been shown to them,

some still do not believe in the threat of the Wurm." The silver-haired woman looked to Cassandra, her eyes filled with intensity. "Some actually believe it to be some sort of conspiracy put in motion by the Cade boy in order to turn us against one another."

"That's insane."

"Yes, isn't it?"

Cassandra was furious; how dare they act this way in a time of crisis? She was about to demand that they stop acting like children, when a booming voice filled the chamber.

"Brothers and sisters of Parliament, I bring you grave news!"

From an entrance at the back of the chamber, a man stumbled toward them. His clothing was in tatters and appeared to be burned in places.

"Who?" she whispered, not realizing that she had spoken aloud.

"A parliamentary scout," the Voice replied. "I sent him to the south, along with four others, to verify the existence of the Wurm threat."

The man stumbled toward them, falling to his knee before the Voice. Cassandra could see a look of terror in his eyes as he gazed about the room. The chamber was abuzz, the appearance of the scout enough to distract those who had been locked in raging arguments mere seconds before.

"What is it?" the Voice inquired. "Share what you have seen so that we may all come to understand the danger we face."

The man grabbed his head as if in agony. "It was horrible. . . ." He gasped. "From Tora'nah they are advancing . . . the Wurm are traveling north . . . traveling toward Arcanum!"

Lord Foxheart, Grandmaster of the Malleus Guild, left his seat, stepping into the aisle so that he might be noticed, his ratlike features contorted with disdain and anger. "What proof do you have, other than your word?"

The room again erupted into frenzy, but Lord Foxheart quickly silenced them. "The Malleus Guild headquarters in Taboluth is located northeast of Tora'nah and as of now, I have heard nothing of this Wurm advancement."

The scout rose to his feet, face lined with fear. "It's not there anymore!" he cried, grabbing his head again as if to keep it from breaking apart.

Foxheart seemed not to understand.

"What do you mean?" he asked. "I don't understand what—"

The scout rushed up the aisle. "Listen to me. It's gone . . . the Malleus Guild headquarters is gone . . . destroyed by the Wurm as they progress north."

Foxheart went white, his mouth agape. All the argument was drained from him.

"Listen to me, all of you!" the scout shouted, stumbling in a circle, trying his best to be certain that every guild member could hear his warning. "The Wurm are coming, of this there is no doubt, and they are stronger than we first imagined. Much, much stronger."

With his warning finally spoken, the scout's eyes rolled back in his head, his body went limp, and he fell unconscious in the middle of the aisle.

The meeting chamber fell silent.

CHAPTER SIX

Still clinging to the back of the stolen prison transport, Ivar lost himself deep in meditation. His muscles burned with effort, his mind with the need to sleep. His whole body seemed to itch. Hunger and thirst assailed him. But with his meditation he was able to retreat within himself, to separate himself from those physical troubles. It was necessary if he was to hold on.

But he knew that he could not hold on indefinitely. He had thought Grimshaw might land to find something to eat or drink, but it was clear the mage was driven by obsession and would not stop until he had reached his goal. Ivar had no choice. He would cleanse his mind and relax his body through meditation, and as soon as the purification of his thoughts was complete, he would find his way into the transport. He could not wait until Grimshaw reached the Wurm invaders. He had to force Grimshaw to bring the craft down to land.

Ivar's eyes snapped open, senses alert to a sound that seemed to come from all around him; a sound only too familiar. The flapping of leathery wings. His flesh reacted quicker than thought, darkening the surface of his skin so that he would blend with the hull of the transport.

Grimshaw would not need to travel all the way to Tora'nah to meet with the Wurm, it seemed. Raptus's army was already moving north, and far more swiftly than Ivar would have expected.

The Wurm darted through the air around the transport, harrying the vehicle, preparing either to force Grimshaw to land or to burn him out of the sky. Ivar was grateful that he was invisible to them, at least for the moment. He felt his warrior's blood pulse in his veins, but there was nothing he could do at that moment, trapped, clinging onto the back of the craft as the enemy circled its prey.

The transport began to slow and then to halt, hovering over a barren section of rocky hills and skeletal forest.

What are you doing, Grimshaw? The madman had just made their craft an even easier target for the Wurm.

"What have we here, brother?" he heard one of the beasts growl, wings flapping as he hovered in the air before the transport. Another of the Wurm soldiers had joined him, hanging in the frigid air, his own pounding wings keeping him aloft.

"Easy prey," the other snarled, and the two laughed in unison, streams of fire and steam erupting from their mouths and nostrils.

As if their amusement were infectious a third Wurm flying about the craft began to laugh as well, the sound of their humor like stones being ground together. Liquid fire bubbled in their mouths as they prepared to engulf the transport in the flame from their gullets. Ivar experienced a complete sense of helplessness, an emotion that was not common for him, and he felt his rage grow.

He began the prayers to his ancestors that would help him on his way to the life after this one, a life free of fire-breathing lizards and dark wizards.

From the corner of his eye he saw it, another Wurm flying in from the south to join its brethren; only this one appeared much larger. Ivar nearly lost his grip when he recognized the new arrival, head clad in a helmet of black metal, fire like lava dripping from his maw.

Raptus.

"What do we have here?" Raptus thundered, as he darted back and forth in front of the craft.

Ivar narrowed his eyes. Though he could not pinpoint what, precisely, it seemed to him that there was something different about the Wurm. He had encountered Raptus in the hellish realm of Draconae, where he had briefly been imprisoned in the volcanic city of the Wurm.

"The afternoon meal," one of the soldiers muttered, snickering under his breath, smoke rising from his nostrils.

Raptus sneered, opened his jaws, and let loose an enormous gout of flame that engulfed the soldier in midflight. The soldier shrieked in pain as the flames spread across his skin, charring his wings. Unable to stay aloft, the burning Wurm spiraled down, down and down, leaving an oily trail of smoke in his passing.

"This is a time for war," their general snarled, looking at the other soldiers flying about the transport. "There is nothing at all amusing about that."

Then it dawned on Ivar why Raptus seemed different. The Wurm commander was somehow larger, his wingspan wider, the scarlet armor that adorned him seemingly too small for his overly muscular frame.

How odd, Ivar thought.

"You fools are wasting time with a single craft!" Raptus bellowed at his soldiers. "Incinerate it!"

The two Wurm soldiers snarled and clicked their tongues in primal communication. They roared to one another and then began a sweeping arc that would bring them around in a moment to the transport. Already the furnaces inside of them were burning, fire streaming out of their jaws.

Ivar steeled himself. If Grimshaw did not do something in a second or two, he was going to have to throw himself off the transport and hope that the fall did not kill him. Just as he was about to jump, the door on the side of the transport banged open, and the former constable emerged.

"General Raptus, wait!" Grimshaw shouted. "Call off your warriors! I wish to parley!"

Raptus laughed, but at the very last moment he waved off the raiders and they veered aside, coming round to wait, wings beating the air.

"I am Raptus, son of Tarqilae. I would sooner parley with demons than with a mage. But I confess I am curious. A lone mage traveling toward the invading horde rather than away. You have half a minute to explain. Half a minute before you die screaming."

"And grateful for it, General," Grimshaw said, his voice raised to be heard over the flapping of Wurm wings. "I am Arturo Grimshaw—a fugitive from the so-called justice of the Parliament of Mages, and I bear you no ill will. On the contrary, I think that I might be very useful to you. We both desire vengeance, Raptus. I would be more than happy to deliver all of Parliament into your clutches."

Raptus tilted his head to one side, sunlight glinting off his helmet as he scrutinized the mage. "A fugitive? Your craft appears to be a cargo transport of some kind; what does it carry?"

"It was supposed to carry me to prison," Grimshaw replied, touching his chest with his flesh-and-blood hand. Ivar noticed that the crackling magical arm was no longer present and understood that the mage did not want to present any sort of threat to Raptus. "As I told you, sir, I am a fugitive, and have come in search of you, for I do believe we share similar views about the ruling powers of Terra."

A Wurm with a horribly scarred face spiraled down from the clouds. Ivar recognized this new arrival from his time on Draconae. "Give the word, General, and we'll burn this pink-skinned fool and his craft from the sky."

Raptus raised his taloned hand. "Patience, Hannuk."

The general glided closer, and Ivar could smell the foul stink of the great beast. His nostrils filled with the acrid stench of burning heatstone.

"You say you are a criminal," Raptus said, addressing Grimshaw. "Tell me, what is your crime?"

Ivar's ears pricked up. He was curious to hear how the man would answer. He doubted that Grimshaw would share that he served the archmage, Alhazred, the mastermind behind the Wurm banishment to Draconae.

"I was a former constable of the law that did not approve of the existence of a dangerous boy named Timothy Cade."

From where he watched, Ivar could see the physical reaction of the Wurm general. Raptus's black lips pulled back from his razor teeth, and his eyes went wide beneath his helm.

"I see, General, that you are familiar with him as well."

Raptus slowly nodded.

"I believed that the abomination should have been destroyed," Grimshaw continued. "But Parliament sided with the freak of nature, and thusly I was sentenced to rot in prison." The former constable stroked the ends of his mustache. "As you can imagine, I no longer hold any allegiance to my former masters; in fact, I would rather like to see them, as well as the boy, destroyed."

Ivar could not believe what he was hearing. He knew Grimshaw to be evil, but he never imagined how loathsome the man could be. If he had the opportunity, he would have killed the mage just then. If there was one thing that made his blood boil with fury, it was treachery.

Raptus made a low, chuffing noise in his throat, little bursts of flame spitting from his snout as he ruminated upon Grimshaw's words. After several moments he turned to Hannuk. "Bring the mage. If he served Parliament, he may hold secrets that will be useful to us."

Hannuk gestured to the two Wurm soldiers. They flew at Grimshaw and roughly plucked him from inside the transport, carrying him off as easily as a hawk carried away its rodent prey.

"What of the craft?" Hannuk asked.

Raptus had been gliding down into the forest below. He did not look up or change course at all, but his shouted command echoed up to the heavens.

"Burn it from the sky."

With several violent beats of his broad wings, Hannuk flew up in front of the transport, opened his jaws and spewed liquid fire that engulfed the craft. Ivar was at the back of the transport, protected from immediate harm, so he hung on as Hannuk let loose another blast of roaring fire. The transport began to burn quickly and listed to one side. Ivar held on with all his strength, so that he wouldn't fall to the ground. Still maintaining his physical camouflage, he climbed onto the transport's roof. The front of the vehicle was completely engulfed in flames that crackled and popped as they consumed metal and wood alike, fire crawling across the roof to where he now crouched. It would be almost certain death for him to leap from this height, but he saw no other alternative.

Satisfied that his task had been completed, Hannuk bent his head and tucked his wings against his back, knifing through the air as he pursued General Raptus and the other Wurm. Others appeared from the clouds above, sentries that Ivar had not noticed before, and they whipped through the air, passing the burning transport on the way down. He counted five all told, and he wondered how many others were down on the forest floor, or flying among the trees . . . how many in the invasion force.

The last of the Wurm that were following Hannuk paused, then circled the blazing transport, which now hung at an angle in the air, fiery debris falling from it to tumble into the forest below. This final straggler seemed strangely captivated by the sight of the burning craft. From what Ivar could tell, the Wurm soldier appeared young, and seemed to relish the sight.

A violent tremor passed through the hull beneath the Asura's feet and something groaned and snapped loudly from inside the transport. The magic would soon disperse from the burning vehicle, and nothing would prevent it from falling from the sky to earth.

Ivar could think of no other way to survive this. He braced himself, standing in the only spot where fire had yet to burn. The heat of the craft's skin beneath his feet was growing more intense, fueling his intentions. He dropped into a crouch, tensing his muscles. He reached for the knife within the sheath hanging from his belt, plucked it free, and with nary a thought he sprang from the surface of the sky craft to land upon the back of the Wurm soldier.

The beast let out a roar of surprise.

Ivar lay flat on its back, allowing its wings the freedom to flap so that they could stay aloft, and pressed the tip of his knife blade against the softer skin located just beneath the Wurm's jaw line.

"Calm yourself, Wurm," Ivar whispered in its ear. "I mean you no harm and only require a means of transport to the ground below."

The Wurm continued to thrash, spinning itself around in the air in an attempt to dislodge its attacker. Ivar held fast, pressing the knife point deeper into the Wurm's throat, this time deep enough to draw blood.

"I *will* end your life before I allow you to dislodge me," he warned, and the Wurm gradually began to calm, soaring around the burning sky craft as the magic at last left its wreck of a body, and it began to fall from the sky in flaming pieces.

"Now take me down," Ivar ordered.

The young Wurm soldier was brash, but not a fool. He did exactly as he was told.

Cassandra couldn't stand the constant bickering anymore.

She had left the Parliament chamber where argument, even though it was disturbingly obvious that this threat was against them all, had continued to reign. Quarreling ran rampant among the grandmasters, ranging from the types of spells and incantations to be used to defend the city to what color uniforms the combat mages should wear to indicate their allegiance. It was almost as if they argued just for the sake of it, and she could bear it no longer.

The Xerxis was enormous, filled with winding corridors and high-ceilinged rooms that practically invited Cassandra in to rest her weary mind. Some almost succeeded, particularly one room that looked onto a lush garden. She would have loved nothing better than to walk the garden and lose herself in the rich greenery and invigorating fragrances of the wonderful place, but duty called.

Through inquiries to various building sentries, she located the section of the Xerxis where the SkyHaven staff had been quartered and went to check on them. Everything appeared to be in order, Carlyle running things with amazing efficiency as always. The Order of Alhazred would continue to function from here, in their makeshift headquarters, until the threats were dealt with and SkyHaven had been inspected for any more potentially dangerous secrets.

Relieved that their resettlement was going so smoothly and her presence was unnecessary at the moment, Cassandra slipped out a side entrance to wander the fabulous hallways and corridors of the Xerxis again. For a moment she felt pangs of guilt for not devoting herself one hundred percent to the approaching threat, but she had done much since the revelation that the Wurm were heading north and deserved a momentary respite.

Edgar had brought word from the Cade estate that Verlis had survived the invasion at Tora'nah, along with some of the workers from the Forge and the mines there. The idea that they had crossed through Draconae to get back to Arcanum with a warning filled her with dread and awe. That sort of courage was precisely what would be required to face Raptus and his army.

A painful knot began to form in the pit of her stomach as she recalled the bird's report of a Wurm secret weapon, something that Raptus may have been looking for at Tora'nah. *What had he called it? The Spawn of Wrath?* Whatever it was called, it filled her with foreboding.

Before the rook had departed, Cassandra had conveyed to Edgar the facts about their relocation from SkyHaven, and the most recent information about the sad fate of the Malleus Guild, and how the Wurm indeed seemed to be moving northward.

Now she paused in her wandering and looked around. She hadn't been paying attention to where she was going, just letting her feet guide her, but now Cassandra found herself in the center of an open lobby. In each of the four corners of the vast chamber was a large marble staircase leading up into an area lit by lanterns of ghostfire. She experienced nagging pangs of pity on seeing the flickering lights.

When things had at last calmed down, she planned to voice her concerns about the use of the soul energies of deceased mages. Though it had been used for centuries as a source of illumination, Cassandra felt that after what she had learned in her and Timothy's recent dealings with

Alhazred, it might be time to put this particular practice to rest. She could just imagine the furor that would surely be stirred up in Parliament over this; but that was a worry for another time.

Cassandra stood at the bottom of one of the four large staircases, peering up into the gloom at the top of the steps. *These stairs must lead to chambers located inside the four corners of the Xerxis tower,* she thought, remembering the spectacular view that she had seen from her sky carriage that morning as they approached. She had never realized that the towers were anything more than ornamental in design, and found herself drawn up the marble staircase.

The stairs began to writhe beneath her feet, and she gasped in surprise. The stairs were moving on their own accord, undulating in such way that she was gently transported up the vast staircase with no effort on her part, higher and higher into the tower. There was more to these stairs than even she imagined, but they were so many and so steep that she was glad they had been enchanted, and that she did not have to climb them on her own.

As she reached the top of the moving staircase, Cassandra saw that a sentry was posted, a female who seemed to be awaiting her arrival.

"Mistress Cassandra," the guard said, bowing at the waist. "Mistress Borgia is waiting for you in the watchtower." She gestured toward yet another staircase that, if she was not mistaken, would take her up into the enormous stone cap that sat atop the ancient building, dwarfed only by the spire that rose up from the parliamentary chambers next door. "Thank you," she said, approaching the stairs. Curiosity drove her up the staircase, which narrowed as she climbed higher, and at the end there was a golden door, and on the door there had been carved the shape of an eye, closed in rest.

Cassandra tentatively passed her hand across the front of the sleeping eye, believing it to be a part of its locking mechanism, but the eye in the door did not recognize her, and thus did not open.

"Hello?" she called, preparing to wrap her knuckles on the door's surface, but before her hand could fall, the eye carved into the door came open to reveal a now staring orb.

"Enter the watchtower, Grandmaster of the Order of Alhazred," the voice of the door said, and it swung wide to allow her access.

Cassandra passed through the doorway and into the spherical chamber that sat atop the residential building just beside the spire of Xerxis. Everywhere her eyes fell, she found mirrors of all shapes and sizes, hanging weightlessly in the air. As she stepped farther into the room, she noticed that each mirror reflected a different part of Arcanum. She recognized the market place, the quadrangle at the University of Saint Germain, one of the many bustling neighborhoods located at the bottom of August Hill.

"What is this place?" she asked aloud, moving toward a particular mirror with a beautifully detailed frame of carved flower blossoms floating at eye level, which showed a pleasant scene of children playing in the street in front of their home.

"It *is* the Watchtower, Cassandra," a woman's voice said in response, and she turned to see Alethea Borgia walking among the floating mirrors, coming toward her.

"It's . . . it's wonderful," she found herself saying, her attentions going back to the playing children.

"It is, isn't it?" the woman answered wistfully. "It was originally created by the founding members of Parliament as a tool to spy upon those who did not agree with the edicts sent down by the leaders of the original thirteen guilds. Today, as you can see, all the mirror eyes are turned toward our capital city."

Alethea lifted her arm and presented the room to Cassandra. "This is what we are trying to preserve—to protect from harm, the day-to-day lives of our citizenry."

Cassandra found her attentions jumping from mirror to mirror, taking in the many sights, and something began to grow disturbingly apparent. Combat mages from various guilds, constables, and acolytes, wearing the insignias and colors of their orders, could be seen moving about the city in preparation.

Cassandra turned to the old woman, realizing what it was that the guild members were monitoring.

"Not all of us are using this time to bicker," the Voice said with a sigh. "Measures had to be taken. Preparations have to begin if we are going to be ready."

Alethea came to stand beside Cassandra, and the two of them observed the mirrors together.

"So much worth defending," the Voice of Parliament said as she gazed about the room.

Cassandra couldn't have agreed more. She glanced across multiple scenes of preparation reflected on the mirror surfaces, taking it all in. This was what being a grandmaster was truly about, of that she had no doubt.

"Mages from many of the service specialties—navigation, architecture, medicine—have all been called upon to aid us in our time of need," Alethea continued. "It will be the constables, combat mages, and guild acolytes who will be our protection if the Wurm are not stopped before reaching Arcanum—if our first line of defense is not successful."

The Voice approached a mirror focused on the lobby of the tower, which explained how the sentry had known that Cassandra was coming up to the watchtower. The silver-haired woman waved her hand in front of it, and the image began to shimmer like water in a pool, its focus changing to another scene altogether.

Cassandra recognized almost immediately the old home perched precariously atop August Hill as the Cade estate. She had never been there, but Timothy talked about his home so often that it was almost as if she had.

"Here are those who will make a difference," Alethea said.

In the mirror Cassandra saw darkly colored sky carriages bearing the crest of the Legion Nocturne hovering in front of the estate. The sky around the old house was filled with Wurm in flight, and for a moment, she was gripped with fear, but then remembered that the clan of Verlis lived at the Cade estate.

Looking closer she saw Lord Romulus, Verlis, and his mate,

Cythra, stepping from the home onto the stone steps that came down from the door and ended in open sky. Sky carriages waited to carry them away. Then Timothy emerged from the house and Cassandra took a sharp breath, smiling softly, her heart glad to see him, even though she could not be with him. He was the last to leave, Edgar flapping above his head as the boy closed the door behind him.

"They travel to the south," Alethea said. "To the fortress of Twilight to gather the forces of the Legion Nocturne and other allies in the region. They will form the first line of defense against Raptus and his army."

As if to reflect the emotions Cassandra was experiencing at that very moment, every one of the mirrors hanging within the watchtower flickered momentarily, all the images suddenly reflecting the group climbing into the sky crafts on August Hill, departing for their mission.

"Safe journey, champions of Terra," Alethea proclaimed. "Our strength and courage added to yours. We shall forever hold you in our minds, and in our hearts for what you are to do. Come back to us."

"Come back to me," Cassandra whispered softly under her breath.

Sheridan's good-byes to his friends still echoed in the foyer of the Cade estate. The mechanical man stood before the door, the memory mechanisms of his clockwork brain replaying the image of Timothy as he prepared to leave on his journey.

"I want you to stay here," Timothy had instructed him. "Someone needs to look after the Wurm children while their parents come south with us."

Sheridan had been taken aback by the request, for he had been prepared to go with them to Twilight, to aid them in any way that he could in their struggles against Raptus and his advancing horde.

It was not like him to argue, but the mechanical man did just that, questioning his master's decision. "Surely I can be of *some* help," he had said, having no desire to be left behind.

The boy had come to him then, a comforting smile on his handsome features. Timothy was growing older, the contours of his face starting to change as he progressed toward adulthood. In his slowly changing features, Sheridan saw the resemblance to his father, and had no doubt that Timothy would grow up to be as great, or an even greater man than Argus Cade had been.

Timothy had placed a hand upon his metal shoulder and looked directly into his optical sensors. "You are helping," he had said earnestly. "Each of us has an important part to play in this, and your part is to make sure that the children of Verlis's clan are safe and secure. It's a very important job, and I'm entrusting it to you."

And Sheridan had begrudgingly understood, accepting his friend and maker's wishes, accepting his part in the greater scheme of things. But it hadn't made it any easier to watch as his best friend walked out the door to confront a fate unknown.

Over the years since his creation, Sheridan had developed the ability to imagine, his mechanical brain able to conjure up all manner of possibilities. It was a function he had grown to appreciate, thinking about the future and the wonders that could await him, his friends, and the world in which they lived.

At that moment, standing perfectly still in the lobby of the Cade estate, Sheridan, the mechanical man, wished that he had the ability to turn this function off. His imagination had started to run wild, images of the Wurm attack on Arcanum filling his whirring head with visions of horror and destruction—visions of what could be if Timothy and the others were not successful.

He was scaring himself, his inner mechanisms starting to work all the harder. There was a consistent, high-pitched whistle emanating from the valve atop his head, but no matter how hard he tried, he could not remove the frightening thoughts from his mechanical brain.

And then he heard the sounds from behind him. The fluttering sounds of multiple sets of young wings, and he turned his head completely around to see the Wurm children silently perched atop the wooden banisters and around the staircase leading to the upper levels, watching him. There were nearly twenty of them—all shapes and sizes, some so young that their wings had not yet developed enough to bear their weight, and they needed to be carried by the older children.

Sheridan looked into their young, dark eyes and recognized what he saw there. Their young minds were filled with the same fearful images as his own.

Each of us has an important part to play in this.

Now the memory of Timothy's words spurred him to action. Sheridan erased the imaginings of an unsure future from his mind and turned his attention to those who had been left in his charge. His friend was depending on him— the children were depending on him. It was his job to chase away their fears, to make them feel safe and secure.

"So," he said to them in his cheeriest of tones as he clapped his metal hands together, rubbing them eagerly. "Who wants to play a game?"

It was a responsibility that Sheridan did not take lightly.

CHAPTER SEVEN

The sojourn to the south had begun with six sky carriages bearing the crest of the Legion Nocturne. By the time the force had left the city of Arcanum, others had joined Lord Romulus's band, swelling the number to more than a hundred flying craft. There were combat mages and acolytes from the Sectus Guild and the Spiral Order, as well as the Malleus Guild. This last had surprised Timothy, but Lord Romulus had explained that with their city-state to the south destroyed, honor demanded that those members of the Malleus Guild in Arcanum be among the first to confront the advancing forces of the Wurm.

The boy rode in the lead carriage with Lord Romulus. They were alone except for Edgar, and the rook did not like the Nocturne Grandmaster very much, so he kept uncharacteristically silent on the trip. Up on the high seat of the sky carriage was Caiaphas. Though the navigation mage was technically in service to the Order of Alhazred, upon the death of Leander Maddox he had unofficially declared himself in service to Timothy in particular. They had endured much together, and Caiaphas had insisted that no one was going to drive the boy anywhere but him. Lord Romulus had argued, but only for a moment. He trusted Caiaphas, and allowed the navigation mage to guide his carriage instead of his usual navigator.

As they soared high above the forest to avoid any sort of surprise attack from below, Timothy glanced out the window. Verlis and Cythra led a force comprised of every adult in their clan. They were the vanguard of the army that Arcanum had deployed southward, flying out ahead of the sky carriages, wings riding the wind and trails of smoke and fire streaming from their jaws.

"They're hideous," Lord Romulus said, breaking a long silence that had descended on them during the ride. "Monstrous to look at."

Timothy smiled. "Actually, I think they're sort of beautiful. I'd love to be able to fly. There's a kind of nobility to them too."

"Caw!" Edgar said softly. And then he muttered, "As long as they're on our side, they're gorgeous!"

Lord Romulus looked up at the sound of the bird's voice, eyes alight within the shadows of his massive helmet. The sky carriage itself was enormous, twice the size of any Timothy had been in, to accommodate the gigantic Grandmaster. Romulus nodded toward Edgar.

"Put that way, master rook, I should have to say I agree with you. Indeed, I'd have no use for miners and blacksmiths under my command if Telford and his workers hadn't proven their valor. I'll assign beauty to any mage or beast willing to stand with us against the invaders."

Timothy uttered a soft laugh. "I'm not sure how Walter Telford would feel to hear you call him beautiful, Lord Romulus."

The giant crossed his arms. "His courage is his beauty, boy, as I'm sure you know. And there is beauty in the skills of the smiths who crafted the armor and weapons they now wear. I only wish we had enough to outfit thousands of mages instead of dozens."

The humor of a moment before had departed and a grim shadow settled on them there in the carriage. Telford and his workers had been honored to ride in a sky carriage as part of the Legion Nocturne's regiment. Particularly as Romulus's guild almost never used sky carriages, preferring the massive horses that they bred, patrolling the region around their mountain fortress on the backs of those grand animals. Timothy had half expected them all to go south on horseback, but Romulus had instead ordered the sky carriages brought from the Legion Nocturne's regional office in Arcanum. They were swifter, and speed was of the essence now.

Timothy thought again of the miners and smiths. Most of the armor and weapons they'd made were back in Arcanum, distributed by order of the Voice to the most accomplished combat mages in the city and to several grandmasters who were going to be at the forefront of any city defense. What armor those workers had worn back from Tora'nah, had been freely given, leaving Telford and his people far more vulnerable, yet none of them had complained. They understood what was at stake. All that mattered was defeating the Wurm horde.

Yet still they had been determined to come along, to fight alongside combat mages. To do what they could. They had more than earned Lord Romulus's respect.

The panel that separated the interior of the sky carriage from the navigator's high seat slid back, and through it Timothy saw the rich blue of Caiaphas's veil.

"Grandmaster Romulus, Twilight is just ahead," said the navigation mage. "Shall I descend?"

"No," Romulus replied, and Timothy thought he saw the giant's eyes narrow inside the darkness of his helmet. "Fly high above, make a single pass to be sure all is well, and then drop us right in front of the gates."

Caiaphas nodded. His voice was grave. "Very well." Then he slid the panel closed.

Timothy frowned. "We're going to drop from this height?"

Perched on the back of a seat, Edgar ruffled his feathers, tilted his head and stared at Romulus in his armor of metal and leather. But the bird said nothing.

"Caiaphas is capable of it," the Nocturne Grandmaster said. "They all are. They must be. We don't know if the

Wurm are using cunning and stealth or simply rampaging across Sunderland. If any of them are hiding in the forests on my game preserve, we do not want to be ambushed."

Timothy nodded and turned his attention once more out the window. Verlis and Cythra had flown close to their carriage, and Caiaphas must have signaled to them, for he saw Verlis make a gesture—sort of a salute—and then the Wurm all began to drop back, beating their wings and climbing higher, safeguarding the mages' approach toward Twilight.

The sky carriage banked to one side and began to turn. Edgar ruffled his feathers again and hopped a bit, trying to keep his perch. Timothy leaned to one side. Only massive Romulus seemed unaffected by the sky carriage turning at that speed.

As they circled, Timothy looked out the window and found he had a clear view of Twilight far below. On his previous visit he and Caiaphas had come as prisoners on horseback, but the sight of the mountain fortress was no less impressive from the sky.

The road that led through the game preserve toward the massive gates crossed a river that was spanned by an enormous stone bridge. Beyond the bridge was the wall, and beyond the wall the fortress city—the empire of the Legion Nocturne—was built into the mountainside. The stone face of the city was like a hundred castles buried in a landslide, towers and turrets and battlements jutting out from the side of the mountain.

In Timothy's experience, most mages relied on magic for everything in their lives. The Legion Nocturne were different. The rock in their fortress might have been quarried with magic, but the structures had been built by hand. They preferred to forge their own weapons and armor—perhaps another reason Romulus respected Telford and his workers—and to make their own clothing. They farmed and hunted without magic, and rode horses instead of sky craft whenever possible.

They were also fierce warriors, highly regarded not merely for their magical combat skills, but for their hand-to-hand fighting as well. If there was anywhere better for the Parliament to arrange a stand against the invading Wurm horde, Timothy could not think of it. Nor anyone better than Romulus to lead it.

His eyes widened as he noticed that the gates were open. Regiments of combat mages and acolytes were camped on the stretch of land between river and wall. Their banners were flying, a myriad of colors. He recognized the insignias of the Order of the Winter Star as well as Spiral Guild reinforcements and a massive complement of mages from the Fraternitas Guild, a monastic, all-male order whose land was due west of Twilight and who kept almost entirely to themselves. Timothy had had no idea there were so many Fraternitas mages, and though they wore simple, rough brown robes, he was heartened by their number.

"I'd no idea there would be so many," Timothy said.

"Raptus doesn't discriminate, kid," Edgar said, then cawed

in punctuation. "He's here to kill us all. No one can afford to stay out of this war."

Romulus only gazed down at the assembled troops and grunted in satisfaction. They began to sink rapidly through the air, dropping straight down toward the stretch of land behind the wall. The wall served little purpose with the gates open, but Timothy realized why they were not closed. After all, what good were gates and walls against an enemy who would attack from the air?

Just before they landed he spotted a group of mages who were familiar to him. There were perhaps twenty of them, small, almost bestial creatures with skin like dried animal hide, the color of a milknut. They were Cuzcotec, a guild of barbaric mages, and he had met their sort before.

"Cuzcotec," he said, glancing at Edgar. The rook blinked but said nothing. Timothy studied Lord Romulus. "They tried to kill me once, when I first came through to this world."

The Grandmaster of the Legion Nocturne stared at him with red eyes, but his expression was unreadable behind his helm. After a moment he nodded heavily.

"Yes. But now you share an enemy with them. Old enmity must be put aside. The rook is correct. The whole world must stand against Raptus. All mages, united. Old grudges and politics must be put aside."

Timothy wanted to argue. They had tried to kill him, after all. But these were probably not the very same Cuzcotec who had snuck into his father's house that night.

And even if they were, Edgar and Romulus were correct. They would make their stand here, in Twilight. They would stop the invaders here, before they ever reached Arcanum.

He admired the towers and battlements of Twilight as they came to a landing, and forced himself to think only of today's enemy, and to forget yesterday's.

Black smoke rose from the ruins of the settlement of the Lake Dwellers, drifting across the sky like the dying exhalations of a thunderstorm. The stilted huts that had been built rising up out of the lake had burned and collapsed into the water, leaving charred posts jutting from the surface. Of the houses that lined the lake, however, nothing remained but embers and smoke.

And most of the Lake Dwellers were little more than ash and bone.

Grimshaw stood on the lakeshore and stared at the smoking ruin, much of it still glowing with dying fire. Perhaps two dozen Wurm flew overhead, circling the lake and the destroyed settlement. Raptus had sent at least that number north and westward as scouts. The rest of his army were spread out around the lake. Some of them were bathing in the water, some were resting, some were simply talking low among themselves about their triumphant march across Sunderland.

The others were herding prisoners.

The Lake Dwellers who had been in the water or on the shore at the time of the attack had escaped the immolation of those who had been indoors and had suffered the rain of fire from the Wurm. Some of them had tried to fight. Those had been attacked more directly. The Wurm all had rudimentary magic, and the Lake Dwellers were no more skilled, but when the dragonkin swooped down from the skies with their jaws wide and talons slashing, the Lake Dwellers had stood no chance. It had been a massacre.

The few Wurm sorcerers had remained in the sky, watching over the entire proceedings, as though they wished to conserve their strength for more important battles ahead. It was good strategy. Precisely what Grimshaw would have done.

But he would not have slaughtered the Lake Dwellers. They had been his allies and faithful servants of Alhazred. He looked forward to seeing the same sort of carnage visited upon the Parliament of Mages, even the entire city of Arcanum. The fools had betrayed him and succumbed to the influence of the accursed Timothy Cade.

The stump of his severed arm itched. The magic that he could manifest into a new arm, a purplish black tentacle of arcane power, always made the scar tissue there tingle. The Parliament had stood by and watched the Wurm, Verlis, bite that arm off at the command of the Cade boy, and they had done nothing. Grimshaw had been the one punished.

He wanted vengeance on them for the insult and for their stupidity. But he had never wished for his allies by the lake to come to an end as horrible as this. Grimshaw set his jaw, grinding his teeth, as he watched the remaining Lake

Dwellers pushed together in a group in the midst of the carnage and wreckage of their encampment. The Wurm seemed to be enjoying their role as shepherds, belching gouts of fire or slicing the air with their talons if any of the Lake Dwellers tried to resist.

Out on the lake, perched on a charred and blackened beam from the home of the Lake Dwellers' chief, was General Raptus.

Grimshaw didn't want to look at him. Something was happening to Raptus and he found it extremely troubling. The Wurm general seemed to be growing, easily twice the size of the smaller Wurm. His helmet had barely fit him and he'd had to crack it off like a milknut shell. And the magic . . . Grimshaw could *feel* the enchantment emanating from him, could practically smell it in the air around the maniacal tyrant. Raptus was not merely their general, he was somehow different from the other Wurm.

He was changing.

Grimshaw found it unsettling.

One of the Lake Dwellers cried out in anguish and rushed at the Wurm soldiers who were prodding and mocking him. He tried to summon a defensive spell but it was pathetic. A pair of Wurm—two females—spewed liquid flame and burned him to tatters.

The commotion drew Raptus's attention. Out on the lake, he turned to look toward the survivors and then spread his wings. His wingspan was almost twice his height, and Grimshaw felt his heart clutch with real, primal fear. Raptus flew the short distance to shore and alighted on the ground, then marched toward where his soldiers herded the surviving Lake Dwellers. He glanced into the sky as though to assure himself nothing was amiss, saw his warriors still flying their circular pattern, and then turned his attention once more to the simple mages of the lake.

But he would not speak to them. Instead he turned and beckoned. "Grimshaw!" he called. "Come here!"

Grimshaw could do nothing but obey. He had allied himself with this monster and he would not allow himself to regret it. Whatever losses were suffered along the way, whatever blood had to be shed, whatever trust had to be broken, it would be worth it to see his vengeance fall in blood and fire upon Arcanum.

He lifted his chin defiantly and strode over to join Raptus.

Some of the Lake Dwellers recognized him and began shouting out to him to save them, to do something, but others saw him for what he was and spat filthy names at him, full of venom and hate. He was a traitor, after all.

"Tell me once more, Grimshaw," Raptus said, not bothering to look at the one-armed mage but instead gazing at his prisoners. "To the north?"

With a sigh Grimshaw nodded. They had been over this many times, discussed all of Arcanum's defenses, the number of guilds, which of the guilds would likely be willing to fight and which would be foolish enough not to take the threat seriously until it was too late.

"Arcanum is still quite a ways away, General. The next settlement to the north is that of the Legion Nocturne. Their grandmaster, Lord Romulus, is a mighty warrior, but he is arrogant. He considers his city and the lands around it an empire, though it's hardly large enough to have been called a kingdom in days of old. Still, if Parliament wishes to mount any defense before you reach the city of Arcanum itself, it will likely come from there. Romulus will gather what forces he can—which could be considerable—and attempt to destroy you."

Raptus's leathery flesh was swollen beneath his armor, which had cracked in several places from the pressure of his growth. He nodded his enormous head, yellow eyes thoughtful.

"And the Parliament?"

Grimshaw sneered. "They don't trust one another enough to mount a truly coordinated defense of an entire city."

If the Wurm could smile, he thought that might explain the strange twist of Raptus's lips, the baring of fangs, the narrowing of the eyes. Then the tyrant turned and gestured toward the surviving Lake Dwellers.

"And these? You'd said they were once your allies."

"Once," Grimshaw agreed.

"Have you no loyalty to them now?"

Grimshaw stood straighter, raised his chin higher, and from the stump of his severed arm emerged that purplish black tentacle of magic that formed itself into a replacement limb, a fist of hatred and sorcery.

"I care only for vengeance now, General Raptus. And my only loyalty is to he who can deliver that vengeance to me."

Raptus spread his wings, turning so swiftly that Grimshaw cried out and staggered back, the dark magic of his sorcerous arm splitting instinctively into several tentacles to protect himself. But the tyrant was not attacking Grimshaw.

With a roar like the earth splitting, Raptus opened his jaws and a torrent of liquid fire rushed out, incinerating the surviving Lake Dwellers where they stood. The other Wurm who had been guarding them only stepped back and watched as their leader murdered their prisoners. Some of them tried to flee, only to fall in flames.

Grimshaw watched in horror. Soon only scorched bones remained.

Raptus made a chuffing noise that might have been laughter. "Well," he said, "it's a good thing you had no loyalty to them, isn't it?"

Hatred brewed in Grimshaw, and he wanted to lash out at Raptus, but his hate for the Parliament and the Cade boy was even more powerful, and so he did not strike.

"Silence?" Raptus said, turning to look down on him. "Ah, well, a little silence from you will be most welcome."

Even as he completed his insult, Raptus grunted in pain. He winced as a spasm passed through him, and then a low moan burbled up from inside his chest, fire gushing from his nostrils. Grimshaw frowned, wondering what was happening, but before he could even ask, Raptus doubled over in agony and let out a roar, clutching his stomach.

"My bones!" he shouted.

"General!" said one of his soldiers, rushing toward him. Raptus swept out a hand and knocked the Wurm sprawling to the ground. "Keep away!" he roared.

Then, with a sound like daggers tearing flesh and hammers breaking bones, he began to grow. The previous size increase had been slow and invisible to the naked eye, taking place over hours. Not now. They all stood and watched in astonishment as Raptus screamed and spasmed and stretched—and grew. His crimson armor shattered and fell to the blackened soil in pieces.

When the growth had subsided, Grimshaw guessed his height at more than twenty feet.

"General? How . . . how is this possible?" he asked.

This time he was certain that chuffing sound was laughter. Raptus looked down at him, and Grimshaw could see the utter madness in his eyes, the lunacy brought on by pain and hatred.

"There it is again," Raptus sneered. "That voice, like the buzz of an insect in my ear. I thank you for your insights and your secrets, Grimshaw. But I have no further use for you. I can assure you that the Parliament of Mages will suffer."

Grimshaw's eyes went wide. He began to stagger backward. He raised his arms and tried to shield himself. Tentacles of black magic lunged at the gigantic Wurm.

Raptus opened his maw, lava spilling over his fangs and searing the ground.

Then the fire came.

It was the last thing Arturo Grimshaw ever saw.

And from the forest, his flesh blending with the colors of the trees, Ivar watched Grimshaw die. He had arrived only moments ago and borne witness to the last of the carnage.

Silent, invisible, he turned to the north and began to run.

The attack on Twilight came at dawn the next day. It had been a long, restless night for the troops, camped on the river and on both sides of the wall. The children of the Legion Nocturne and the infirm had been evacuated north to Arcanum, so within the sprawling city built into the mountainside there were only warriors. Sentries were placed upon watchtowers and scouts were sent up to the top of the mountain and across the lands. The Wurm invaders could not reach Twilight without being seen and the sentries would sound a horn that would warn of impending attack. They could sleep in shifts.

Still, Timothy spent a restless night as a guest of Lord Romulus. The moon was bright in the sky outside his window, and each cloud that drifted across it felt to him like the shadow of Raptus himself. He had been in the clutches of the tyrant before—a prisoner on Draconae—and he knew there would be no mercy. Memories of the cruelty in Raptus's eyes, the brutal power of the monster beneath that crimson armor, were etched in his mind.

The night passed with excruciating slowness and though he slipped into sleep from time to time, he would be quickly awakened by a noise in the fortress or outside at the base of the mountain, where the mages gathered to await the war. At last, an hour or so before dawn, exhaustion overcame him, and he was dragged down into a sound, dreamless sleep.

It was not the horns that woke him. Not the rattling of armor and weapons or the shouts of alarm from outside. Timothy would have slept through all of that, if not for Edgar.

The rook cawed and cried, flying about the room.

Timothy's eyelids fluttered open, and he saw that the sky was lightening from black to rich blue, the sun only hinting at the coming day. It took him a moment of staring stupidly at the panicked rook before he actually heard Edgar's words.

"The horn!" the bird snapped. "Get up, Tim! They've sounded the horn! The Wurm are here! It's happening now! Get up!"

Then all the other sounds flooded in. He heard the mournful sound of the warning horns echoing across the mountain fortress and the shouts of mages in preparation. Out in the corridor boots hammered stone, as combat mages of the Legion Nocturne raced outside to take up their positions.

A fist pounded on the door to Timothy's room.

The boy felt his heart thundering in his chest in time with those running footfalls and the pounding on the door. He sprang from the bed and pulled on his boots. He'd slept fully clothed so as to be prepared for attack.

"I'm coming!" Timothy cried in response to the banging at his door.

Edgar still flew in circles, as though he could not pause, and the boy knew how he felt. There would be no rest now. Not until this was over.

"Caw!" Edgar cried. "I don't know what you're doing here! The Wurm aren't mages. Magic won't hurt you, but their talons and their fire will!"

Timothy hesitated at the door, staring at him. "Edgar, don't. We've had this discussion. You said yourself this war concerns everyone. If I can be of any help at all, I have to be here."

Black feathers fluttering, the rook hovered a moment. "You're your father's son."

"I'll take that as a compliment," Timothy said, and he threw open the door.

Walter Telford stood in the corridor. He was grim faced and there were beads of sweat on his forehead. In his hands he held a shirt of silver chain mail and a sword in a gleaming scabbard. Across his back was slung a metal shield.

Timothy frowned. "Walter, what—"

"Hurry and dress in this, Timothy. There isn't time for questions."

The boy took the chain mail shirt and studied it, astonished. "Is this Malleum? It must have taken forever to make something so intricate."

Telford nodded. "Scraps, son, left over from the forging of all the rest of the armor. We collected it as we went and crafted this for you. This world has been cruel to you, Timothy, and those at the Forge wanted you to realize there is a place for you. You may be unique, but you are a brilliant and courageous boy. We hope to help keep you safe if we can."

Timothy was so touched that he could barely breathe. He slipped the chain mail shirt on and then took the sword and shield that Telford offered him. "But . . . this isn't right, Walter. You and your people—you mined and forged all these things—but you fight with iron instead of Malleum. I shouldn't have this if you can't be protected as well."

Telford smiled. "Then protect us, Timothy."

The boy's throat went dry. "I'm no warrior. Not really. Ivar taught me hand-to-hand combat, but against the Wurm—"

The mage tapped him on the head. "A warrior uses more than his hands. Now let's go. The horn sounded minutes ago. The Wurm will be here any—"

Outside there came a new volley of shouting but there was a different tone to the combat mages' voices now. Timothy heard the hum and sizzle of spells being cast.

"They're here!" Edgar shouted.

The rook flew along the corridor to a high arched stone window and settled on the sill. Telford and Timothy ran after him. Streams of fire began to rain from above, and as they looked up, they could see dozens of Wurm silhouetted against the lightening sky. The sun was just beginning to rise, the horizon burning gold.

On the ground the hundreds of combat mages from the gathered guilds joined together. The air crackled with defensive spells, as magical shields were erected to protect them from the fire. If the Wurm wanted to kill them, they would have to descend, to come down and fight the war on the ground.

Then the real bloodshed would begin.

"Let's go!" Timothy said, and he and Telford ran along the corridor together, with Edgar flying close behind.

The boy managed to clip the scabbard to his belt, but he knew he would not need it for very long. The sword would be unsheathed soon enough. He slid the shield onto his left arm, and by that time they were hurrying down the stairs that would take them outside, onto the upper battlements of Twilight. Many of the troops were spread out far below, but the Legion Nocturne were stationed on the towers and walls of their fortress.

Timothy raced out onto the stone battlement with Edgar on his shoulder and Telford hurrying after them. Around them were several Legion Nocturne mages, all of them wearing the metal and leather armor of their guild.

"Here they come!" roared one of the Legionnaires.

Edgar took to the air silently, going up to meet the Wurm raiders that were descending. Their wings seemed to slice the air, and their eyes gleamed in the dawn shadows. Fire and black smoke trailed behind them, slipping from their nostrils and open maws. Three Wurm dove down at the group of combat mages Timothy stood with, and he raised his shield.

They all had magic to protect them, but he had the faith and workmanship of Walter Telford and his men.

One of the Wurm came straight at him, its jaws opened wide, and it let loose a stream of fire. Timothy raised his shield, ducking his head behind it, and the fire was turned harmlessly away. The Wurm was nearly upon him, talons raised.

Edgar screamed as he darted from the west, scratching at the Wurm's eyes, distracting it with pain and surprise. Timothy dodged to one side, his shield taking only a fraction of the impact that would have struck him if he had remained in position. And as the Wurm scrambled to fly away, to get its bearings, he ran to the edge of the stone battlement and—with momentum that would have carried him over and down to his death if he'd missed—drove his sword through the Wurm's chest.

The sword was lodged in the bones of its torso for a moment. As it began to fall, wings pulled tight to its body, dying before his eyes, its weight dragged him forward. Then he felt Walter Telford grab him from behind.

"Let go of the sword!" Telford cried.

But Timothy refused. He held on. The weight of the Wurm pulled on the blade, but then its edges cut bone and the sword was free. The corpse of the Wurm tumbled down, rolling to the bottom of the mountain face. Far below, Timothy saw a small clutch of Cuzcotec. The bestial, murderous mages saw the dead Wurm and looked up at him, then began to cheer.

The combat mages around him were still fighting, casting spells against the Wurm only to have magic and fire hurled at them in return. Then Timothy heard a thunderous roar, a cry of passion, and looked up to see another Wurm coming in. He raised his sword again but this one attacked the other Wurm, bellowing liquid fire at them, burning the nearest and then grappling with him in midair, talons slashing.

Only when he saw the familiar pattern of horns upon her head did he recognize Cythra. Verlis's mate began to tear at her enemy, driving him down toward a lower battlement.

"There are more coming!" Telford shouted.

Edgar cawed, wordlessly voicing the same message. Timothy looked up and saw the others coming over the top of the mountain, and he steadied himself.

It was difficult to tell from below, but he gauged the size of the thing at forty feet, quadruple the size of any other Wurm. The fire that drooled from its gaping maw set the trees on top of the mountain ablaze, and its wingspan was as wide as the monster was tall. There was madness and hunger in its yellow eyes. It began to laugh and the sound was like the distant rumble of a coming storm.

"By the three moons!" Telford shouted. "How can this be? What sorcery could create such a colossus?"

The answer to the question seemed so simple to Timothy. *The Spawn of Wrath,* he thought.

"Raptus," he said, almost under his breath. Then he turned to Telford. "It's Raptus."

That was the moment in which he knew that the troops that had assembled under Romulus's banner were not going to be enough.

We're going to lose.

CHAPTER EIGHT

S houts and screams were all around. The sun was rising
in earnest now and the gigantic Raptus looked almost
like a massive statue come to life. The towering Wurm
launched himself from the mountaintop and took flight.
The air displaced by his beating wings buffeted the fortress
of Twilight. On a battlement off to Timothy's left, a mage
was knocked over the edge by the power of that wind. He
caught himself with a quickly cast spell, otherwise he would
have been dead, dashed against the rocks below.

"By the moons, how do we fight that?" shouted one of
the Legion Nocturne.

Timothy shuddered in fear. If the callous, battle-hard-
ened Legionnaires were afraid, they really were in trouble.

Raptus laughed again as he flew above the gathered
combat mages from the Spiral and Sectus guilds and the
Order of the Winter Star. There were other troops there, but

they were all one force now, all one army standing in resistance to the Wurm onslaught.

But the Legionnaire was right. How could they stand against this?

Working together, a group of combat mages threw up a shield that covered much of the battlefield below. It spread across both sides of the wall and even across the river. Many of the Wurm were on the ground already, fighting hand to hand with the mages, talons drawing blood. Wurm had been killed, but many more of the mages had already died. The mages had far greater numbers, but the Wurm were more ferocious and more physically powerful.

Wurm sorcerers flew above the melee and cast dark magic down into the midst of battle, undoing the protections and wards of the combat mages wherever they could.

Then Raptus struck. He landed inside the gate, at the base of the mountainside fortress. With a single blow he struck out and shattered the open gates and a portion of the wall.

Mages moved in to attack. The Wurm sorcerers did not bother to aid him, and that ought to have been reason enough to worry. It meant that Raptus did not need their help. His entire body, tall as the trees in the forest, seemed to leak dark, blackly shimmering magic. It emanated from him, powerful enough that Timothy could feel it brush the nullifying field his own body produced. A wave of nausea passed through him and he knew, in that moment, what evil felt like.

"Die, deceivers! Die, betrayers!" Raptus roared, and the words shook the very foundation of Twilight. "Die, mages!"

With a wave of his hand, Raptus sent a flash of sickly yellow magic spilling over the combat mages and acolytes that surrounded him there at the base of the mountain. The most powerful of them remained standing, shielding themselves with magic that would have made the Wizards of Old proud. Lord Romulus was among them, tall and strong. The rest were thrown to the ground, disoriented, and Timothy could see their hands moving, gesticulating wildly as they tried to summon attack spells to try to retaliate against Raptus. Some of them succeeded, enchantments bursting to light around their hands. Romulus seemed to carve a ball of bright red light from the air, and it shot at Raptus, but dissipated as it touched the magical aura that burned around the gigantic Wurm. Most of the others were still too shaken to muster much power.

Raptus spread his wings out over them, casting the shadow of death on them, and then he bent down and vomited out a river of churning, viscous fire that swept over the mages around him like a tidal wave. Timothy could see those mages powerful enough to withstand the assault like islands in the firestorm, but dozens died in just a few seconds of fire and hate.

The battle raged on, but he knew then that it was over. Twilight was going to be destroyed, and unless they found a way to retreat, all of her defenders would eventually be killed. They had no choice but to try to escape, to fall back to Arcanum and try to devise a way to defend the city against the Wurm invasion and their leader, transformed by the Spawn of Wrath.

He looked up, searching the skies. Wurm were in aerial combat with Verlis's clan. Cythra was covered in blood, but he didn't think it was her own. She was perhaps three hundred feet above and just to the left. But Cythra was not the object of his search. Timothy kept looking, even as he heard combat mages barking orders.

At last he saw Verlis, twisting through the air, locked in mortal combat with one of Raptus's raiders.

Timothy spun to Telford and Edgar.

"Walter, get back inside. Get downstairs and gather all of the people you can find. No one can remain inside Twilight. Get the mages on the towers and battlements and get them all to join the battle outside. Twilight is lost. The war is out there for the moment."

Telford stared at him. "They'll never listen to me, Tim. I'm just an ordinary mage. I'm no warrior."

"Tell them the order comes from Romulus himself," Timothy snapped.

The stout, gray-haired mage shook his head. "Romulus will kill you."

"You wanted me to use my head to protect your people. That's what I'm trying to do. Trust me!"

Telford hesitated only a moment longer, and then he ran back the way they'd come, entering Twilight and calling for an evacuation. His shouting was swallowed by the stone fortress in an instant, but by then Timothy had turned his attention to his familiar.

"There's Verlis!" he told the rook, pointing into the sky. "Go and bring him here, Edgar. And hurry!"

Timothy raised his sword and shield as he watched Edgar tearing across the sky, a black streak racing toward Verlis and his opponent. Verlis had now spun his enemy around and was clawing at the Wurm raider's wings. Fire spilled from the enemy Wurm's snout as Verlis reached around and broke his jaw. Timothy watched as the injured Wurm plummeted from the sky. High above, Verlis turned at Edgar's approach, the rook a black smear against the sky from this distance.

The boy heard the clatter of nearby combat and turned to see that the two mages still with him on the battlement were trying to fight off a Wurm that had dropped down from above to surprise them. He was about to attack with his Malleum sword when he saw the ball of bubbling orange-brown light that sprang up in the outstretched palm of the Wurm. This was no raider, but one of Raptus's sorcerers.

Lips pressed tightly into a grim line, Timothy sheathed his sword and ran at the beast. He was not in time to prevent it from unleashing its magic. The sorcerer struck one of the Legion Nocturne mages with its brutal war spell. The mage had been focused on the physical fight, wielding a huge ax, and had not been prepared for the magical attack. He screamed as it hit him, the dark magic causing his entire body to shudder. All the moisture seemed to go out of him, and his entire body withered where he stood. He fell, tumbling over the edge of the battlement. The other Legionnaire cried out in fury and anguish and renewed his attack. The mage summoned a spell, sketching at the air with his fingers and chanting ancient words, but he was going to be too late.

Timothy held his shield on his left arm. With his right hand, he reached out and grabbed hold of the Wurm's tail.

The sorcerer's magic winked out like a dying star, as though it had never been. In the moment of its panic and shock, it did not think to use its fire to attack. The remaining combat mage ran it through with his iron sword.

"You!" Timothy shouted. "Orders from Lord Romulus! Withdraw from Twilight immediately. We have to fall back to Arcanum!"

Denial and rage burned in the mage's eyes, but he did not argue. It would be a terrible blow for the Legion Nocturne to have to retreat, but if Lord Romulus commanded it, they would do so.

Now all Timothy had to do was get Romulus to actually issue that command.

The mage disappeared inside one of the arched doorways that led into Twilight fortress. Timothy heard a familiar cawing and turned to see Edgar and Verlis descending. Cythra was right behind Verlis, glancing around as though challenging Raptus's raiders to attack her. But the enemy otherwise occupied, battling those of Romulus's troops that had not yet been destroyed.

"Timothy, you have a plan?" Verlis shouted over the roar

of battle as he alighted at the edge of the battlement.

The boy ran to him. The Wurm's eyes were grim and expectant, but behind him Cythra was distracted, ready to get back to the fight. Edgar landed on Timothy's shoulder, cawing softly, head twitching crazily as he watched for attack.

"We can't win here. Not today. We weren't prepared for what Raptus has become. We've got to try to withdraw with as many of our troops as we can, get word back to Arcanum and try to ready the city. The Parliament will find a way to battle Raptus, but there's nothing we can do here."

Verlis spread his wings, and fire jetted from his snout in anger. He shook his head, but now it was frustration not rage.

"I hate that you speak the truth," he said. "What do you propose?"

"Take me down to Romulus!"

Without waiting for further explanation, Verlis made a rapid clicking noise to Cythra and took wing. With the strong, clawed hands that had just slain one of his own distant kin, he grabbed Timothy beneath the arms and drove them both over the edge of the battlements. Edgar cawed wildly and flew off, trying to keep pace with them. Timothy thought for a moment that they were simply falling, but then he felt Verlis thrust out his wings and arrest their descent.

They soared low over the bone-strewn battlefield. Raptus had moved on, pushing past the walls and attacking a regiment of Sectus mages who faced him boldly from the edge of the river. Already fire was spewing from the gigantic creature's mouth, and mages were dying. From this vantage point, Timothy was even more astounded by the size of Raptus. The monster towered above them.

Around the ruin of the gate a small group of mages had gathered. There were several Spiral Guild mages and at least half a dozen who wore the symbol of the Winter Star. All of them were also clad in Malleum armor and carried weapons of the same metal. There were four Cuzcotec with them, the creatures seeming even smaller now in comparison to Raptus. They were gnarled, weathered mages, no more than four feet tall, and they skipped about like apes. But they were obviously powerful, or they would already have been dead.

Some of that group were attacking Raptus from behind, combining their spellcasting to try to forge a bit of magic that would do some damage to the gigantic Wurm general. Nothing seemed to be working. A small section of Raptus's right wing had been burned and still glowed like embers in a fire, but that was barely a scratch and hadn't even gotten his attention.

Wurm raiders dove from the sky and harried the archmages on the ground. At the lead of those fighting off these Wurm attackers was Lord Romulus. Another figure moved beside him, almost disappearing with each motion, the sunlight seeming to bend around him. If his appearance had not been so unexpected, Timothy would have recognized him right away. But it was only when he saw the black markings shifting across the body of this partially invisible figure that the truth hit him.

"Ivar!" he shouted.

Verlis dropped him at Romulus's side. Timothy drew his sword and began to hack at a Wurm that was about to unleash a blast of liquid fire on the Nocturne Grandmaster. Some of its flame was turned on him, but his shield protected him, even as Lord Romulus—twice Timothy's height—let loose a spell that knocked the Wurm from the air with a cracking noise that sounded as though the attack had broken all of its bones. It tried to rise but cried out in pain, unable to move without agony.

"Boy, what are you doing? You'll be killed out here!"

Timothy ignored him, going to Ivar, who was on a Wurm's back, choking it.

"You're alive!" he called. "Ivar! You're alive!"

The Asura rode the Wurm onto the dirt, where it lay unmoving, and then rose. His skin returned to its natural hue and he smiled, reaching for Timothy. As Ivar embraced him, Timothy felt a spark of hope ignite inside him.

"I forced myself not to even think about you. I didn't dare." Then he pulled back and looked up at Ivar. "What of Grimshaw? Is he allied with Raptus now?"

"Grimshaw is dead."

Lord Romulus roared and leaped in front of them, throwing up a magical shield of shimmering blue energy. A Wurm crashed into the shield and was repelled, stunned.

The thing staggered back and the Cuzcotec jumped on it, long ropy tendrils of sizzling magic choking and binding it. Then Romulus spun on them. "Yes, Grimshaw is dead!" he snapped at Timothy. "Or so the Asura was just telling me. But we've no time for details now. We've got to fight! And you're going to be killed here on the field!"

Verlis roared nearby, and Timothy looked over to see him and Cythra attacking a Wurm that had dropped down on them from above. Edgar was cawing and darting about the Wurm's head to distract it.

"Listen to me!" Timothy shouted at Romulus. "You're wrong. We can't fight. We've got to retreat. All of the mages have to make one concentrated attack on Raptus and stagger him if possible, just enough time to buy us a moment to withdraw."

"What?" Romulus bellowed. "We'll likely all be slaughtered. Look at what he's become!"

"Maybe!" Timothy snapped, looking at both Romulus and Ivar. "But if we stay, we will most *certainly* all be slaughtered. If we can make it back to the city, we can tell them what's happened and hope the Parliament comes up with a way to stop Raptus."

The sky seemed to open up with thunder but it was only the sound of Raptus unleashing another torrent of liquid fire. The banners of the Order of the Winter Star went up in flames as twenty or thirty more mages died.

Romulus hesitated.

"We've got to go now!" Timothy told him, deciding it

would be a mistake to reveal that he had already begun to spread the word of a retreat.

The Grandmaster of the Legion Nocturne looked at Ivar. The Asura nodded. Timothy was right. They both knew it.

Romulus shouted his fury to the sky.

Cassandra rose with the sun, bathed and dressed, planning to go up to the watchtower for a report on city security and to discover if there'd been any word from Twilight. She picked up her brush and stepped out on the balcony. Running the brush through her hair, she gazed out at the city of Arcanum. Her temporary residence in the Xerxis was on the fourth floor and had a view of the broad courtyard in front of the main entrance to the parliamentary compound. If she looked to the right and craned her neck, she could see the great spire atop the Xerxis, but the watchtower was behind her, and she had no view of it from here. To the left there were grand homes and the embassy towers of dozens of different guilds. And straight ahead there rose the spires of elegant residential buildings, houses of faith, and the training centers for hundreds of different tradecrafts. In the distance she could see the hills on the outskirts of the city, August Hill the tallest and most prominent of all.

Arcanum. Her home.

As she brushed her hair, Cassandra let her mind wander, and her thoughts were of Timothy. Without even realizing it, she set the brush down on the balcony rail. Peering into the distance, she fancied that she could see all the way south to Twilight. She knew how foolish it was for her to be so concerned about the fate of one boy when the whole world was in peril, but she could not help it. An image of Timothy's face floated in her mind, eyes alight with the intensity he brought to his inventions and his arguments with Parliament.

Cassandra bit her lower lip.

He would be all right. She couldn't allow herself to consider any other alternative.

"Enough," she whispered to herself.

Smoothing her robes she began to turn to go back into her quarters, but then she saw something just out of the corner of her eye that drew her attention. On the southern horizon, as high as August Hill, there were three dark shapes against the sunlit sky.

Wurm.

Cassandra shook her head slowly. It had to be members of Verlis's clan. Perhaps not all of the adults had gone south with Lord Romulus after all. There was no way—

In the distance she heard a bell begin to ring, a deep, sonorous sound that carried on the light breeze. Another picked up the clangor and then another, and soon every bell in Arcanum was ringing. The three Wurm were flying at incredible speed, passing over the city, headed toward the Xerxis.

The bells were an alarm.

Cassandra spun and ran back through her quarters. She

did not bother with her brush or the doors to the balcony, leaving them wide open to the sunshine and the breeze. Nothing mattered now but action and speed. She slammed the door to her quarters behind her as she raced out into the corridor and then sprinted for the stairs. Other mages were already spilling out of their rooms, some with weapons. She ignored them. Cassandra had to find out what was happening, how large the attack force was, what this meant for their troops at Twilight, and whether or not the city was prepared.

Her right hand clutched an iron rail as she ran down the long spiral staircase that would take her to the first floor. Round and round she descended. As she reached the bottom, she saw several grandmasters rushing toward the heart of the Xerxis, where they might gather in the parliamentary chamber. Cassandra frowned deeply, wondering how the naysayers would explain this. Perhaps, at last, they would realize that they could not deny a crisis when it was happening all around them. But the time when Parliament might have been in control of what was to come had long passed. While they had continued to argue, the decisions were now being made by others. The Voice of Parliament and many of those loyal to her had set a plan in motion with the chief constable of Arcanum and his deputies.

If there was a war council here, it would be in the watchtower. That was where the defense of Arcanum would be organized.

The flow of people—grandmasters and their aides—moved

toward the heart of the Xerxis, toward the parliamentary chamber. Cassandra turned in the other direction, heading for the junction where she would be able to ascend to the watchtower.

Then she heard Carlyle call her name.

She spun to see him running toward her with several acolytes of the Order of Alhazred. Her guild. Her people.

"Grandmaster," Carlyle said, "the city is under attack. The Wurm are here—"

"I'm aware of that!" she said, not meaning to be harsh but not willing to be delayed.

But Carlyle was no longer the fussy assistant that he so often seemed. Once before, she had seen him revert to the hardened, expert combat mage he had been in his youth. Now here he was again, curt and professional, ready for a fight.

"Mistress, I'm sorry, but it is our job to make certain no harm comes to you."

She stared at him in horror. "You expect me to stay out of the battle to defend Arcanum?"

Carlyle flinched. "Not at all, Grandmaster. I'd never suggest it. But you're the Grandmaster of the Order of Alhazred. Your guild will fight at your side. They're assembling outside as we speak."

Cassandra nodded. A smile spread across her features. She glanced once in the direction of the watchtower, but she knew that Alethea Borgia had the defense of the city well in hand. What Arcanum needed were champions to fight for her.

"What are we waiting for?" she asked.

Carlyle smiled and stepped back, letting Cassandra take the lead. He told her where her combat mages and acolytes were gathered, and she ran along a corridor and found the door that led outside. They were there on a broad lawn awaiting her orders.

But all of them were staring into the sky, looking more mystified than concerned.

Only then did she realize that the bells had stopped ringing.

"What's going on?" she demanded.

A combat mage named Tosches turned and, realizing to whom he spoke, stood up straight and nodded respectfully. "Grandmaster. It appears the Wurm have gone."

"Gone?" Carlyle asked, incredulous. "They're not going to just leave Arcanum alone."

"No," Cassandra agreed. "But I saw them. Only three. I'd assumed there were more, but perhaps not. Perhaps they're merely scouts, taking our measure."

Carlyle knitted his brows in thought. "Perhaps. But what of Twilight, then?"

To that, Cassandra had no answer.

Vermin.

To Raptus the mages scurrying around on the ground were nothing but vermin. He was filled to bursting with the magic of the Spawn of Wrath, could feel it pulsing inside of him like the fire in the furnace of his belly, only even more powerful. When he spread his wings, the wind knocked some of them down. Others he crushed underfoot.

All around him his raiders did battle with mages, but he had already realized the truth. General Raptus no longer needed his army. He was an army unto himself. Throughout all the years he had spent darkly dreaming of his return to Terra and his vengeance upon the mages, he had thought only of destruction. Now, though, he had begun to think of conquest. Death would be merciful compared to the cruelty to which the mages had banished the Wurm. They did not deserve death.

No. He would not kill them all. Raptus would fly from city to city, village to village. He would burn and shatter their civilization, and then he would make slaves of them all. They would have no other choice, for how could they stop him?

His kin were all around him, his soldiers, his loyal followers, but he gave them little thought now. Even Hannuk, who led the scouts to the north, was of little consequence to him. His people were free, as he had promised them, and he gave them barely a thought. On the wing, they would continue to serve at his side, to attack the mages, to fight for vengeance. For justice.

But he didn't need them anymore. The Spawn of Wrath had transformed him into something greater.

Raptus stood on the bloodstained field between the gates of Twilight and the river that ran past. He had personally slain at least half the mages who had gathered there to oppose him, his fire engulfing dozens at a time. The magic they hurled at him had staggered him several times, but otherwise they had not harmed him. Even the most powerful mages among them would fall eventually, either by fire or by magic or because Raptus, unable to kill them any other way, would simply tear them apart.

A regiment of mages in blue and gold were retreating across the stone bridge that spanned the river. There were larger groups off to the east and he knew there were many still inside the mountainside stronghold city, but all things in time.

Raptus was the most powerful creature in the world now. The nightmare of Draconae, the insult of banishment, was long behind him. He had nothing but time. Time to kill and time to hate, at his leisure.

The laughter that he seemed unable now to control exploded out of him again and he took several vast steps toward the bridge. The mages who raced across it realized he was coming for them, and many of them turned to defend themselves, attempting to cast a spell that would shield them. Raptus felt the magic crackling all over him and the fire burbling up through his chest, rising in his gullet. He spread his wings wide and bent down to breathe that volcanic fire down upon them—

The magic struck him from behind, a spell of such power that it could only have been conjured and cast by a great many archmages working together. It was a spell of eradication, meant to disintegrate whatever it touched, one of the most savagely powerful spells in existence because it would obliterate anything in its way. It struck Raptus's left wing from the back and the impact spun him around. He roared in pain. Glancing back at the damaged wing, he saw a tattered, ragged hole had been blown right through it, muscle and skin hanging down. Blood rained down upon the soil of Twilight.

Raptus tried to lift his head, meaning to destroy them all, but he fell to his knees, tail sweeping behind him. Still barely able to see through his pain, he raised his head and shot a volley of liquid fire out across the field, immolating anything in his way.

Then the pain began to subside. He felt the magic of the Spawn of Wrath filling him once more, as though he was still too small to contain all the power of the Dragons of Old. When he glanced at the wing again, forcing himself to focus, he saw the flesh and muscle knitting itself back together again. He had not had the strength—the magic—to do such a thing earlier, but now, moment by moment, he grew in size and in power.

Once more Raptus began to laugh.

Staggering, he rose to his feet and looked around.

The mages were fleeing. Sky carriages darted through the air, rushing away from the mountain stronghold of the Legion Nocturne. Twilight was being emptied of troops. Raptus's raiders were pursuing them, attacking, but the combat mages managed for the most part to keep them away.

On the ground, mages were running on foot or riding

horses. Raptus realized he must have been disoriented for longer than he'd thought, for most of them—more than one hundred, he guessed—had already made it across the bridge and were racing for the forest. The Wurm were giving chase, and some of the mages were brought down, but if they were to be kept from escaping, it would be up to Raptus.

He started after them.

At the bridge he stopped and watched them go.

"General!" shouted a Wurm soldier who flew, hovering, beside him. "Aren't we going to stop them?"

Raptus laughed once more, uncontrollably. Then he shook his head. With a single flap of his wings—a spike of pain running through him from his still-healing wound—he carried himself far across the river and along the road away from Twilight.

"Run!" he shouted, his voice as large as his body, carrying like the echo of thunder all across the lands of the Legion Nocturne. "Flee back to Arcanum, cowardly mages! Vermin! Raptus is merciful! You shall have a single day to prepare. When I arrive at the Xerxis, the Parliament of Mages shall surrender to me the city of Arcanum, the nation of Sunderland, and Terra! You will bow before me, or you will die!"

CHAPTER NINE

The atmosphere in the parliamentary chamber that afternoon was entirely different than it had been the previous day. Or any other day in the history of Terra, Cassandra suspected. There was no more bickering, no more shouting. The grandmasters had ceased accusing one another of heresy or treachery and not a single word was spoken that attempted to lay the blame for the troubles facing Arcanum on Timothy Cade.

It was quiet in the spire of the Xerxis. The light that shone down from the window high above seemed to exist only to cast shadows. The first person Cassandra had sought out when the Voice had called this meeting had been Lord Foxheart of the Malleus Guild. Fewer than twenty of the combat mages he had sent to Twilight under Romulus's command had returned alive. In the space of a single day, at least three quarters of the members of the guild—those who looked to Lord Foxheart for leadership—had been killed, and their settlement destroyed.

He was a ghost of a man now. Lord Foxheart seemed to have shrunken into himself.

Cassandra had found him in the moments before the Voice called the chamber to order, and she had touched him gently on the shoulder. His eyes, when he looked at her, were wary. His expression no longer reminded her of a rodent, but instead of a grandfather who has lived long enough to acquire sadness and wisdom in equal measure.

"Grandmaster Nicodemus," Foxheart had begun, "I must offer you an apology. It seems I owe regrets to a great many—"

"No, sir, I beg you," she'd said, holding up a hand. "We are all joined in our grief and determination today. There is only one guild as of this moment. I only wanted to offer my con-dolences."

Lord Foxheart had taken her hand, squeezed her fingers, and nodded once. She thought he might thank her, but then realized that he could not summon the words.

"We will stop them," she said.

"We must," Foxheart had replied. "There is no other choice."

Then the meeting had begun. The Voice of Parliament had entered with Lord Romulus and Verlis. Given that the last time the Wurm had been within the parliamentary chamber he had bitten off the arm of Constable Grimshaw, Cassandra was surprised there was no uproar upon his entrance. To her the lack of opposition was the ultimate example of just how serious their situation had become.

It was declared that Romulus would remain in command of the joint combat forces of the guilds of Parliament. Though the battle of Twilight could be seen as nothing but a disaster, no one debated Alethea Borgia's decision. Given what had become of Raptus, Cassandra considered it nothing short of miraculous that anyone had survived that encounter.

"As I speak to you," the Voice continued, "many nonessential personnel, including thousands of unskilled mages, children, and noncombatant parents, are being evacuated northward. They will have only a small number of combat mages as their guard. We are taking an enormous risk that the Wurm will not simply bypass Arcanum and go on to the north to strike at them. But Verlis has assured us that Raptus's desire for conquest will overpower his bloodlust for the time being.

"At this moment, many hundreds of acolytes from every guild are being put into place on strategic structures throughout the city. They will attempt to attack the Wurm while the enemy are still in the air, and to draw them down for close combat if possible. We have chosen structures that are constructed of fireproof materials or protected by enchantments that will prevent them from burning."

The Voice paused and glanced around the room. Every face was turned toward her, all eyes locked on her. Then she turned to Lord Romulus. "The floor is yours," she said.

Romulus nodded to her, then to Verlis, including him as though he were a visiting dignitary. Which, in many ways, was what he had become.

"My friends . . . ," he began, letting the words resonate throughout the chamber, perhaps allowing the gathered mages get used to the idea that they had indeed come together, for once, as friends. "Your cooperation thus far has been exceptional. I understand how difficult it has been for all of you to cede the direct command over your guilds to the Voice and, as the Parliament's appointed commander, to me. I grieve deeply for the losses many of our guilds have already suffered, and so feel even more keenly the responsibility placed upon me.

"I wish that I could guarantee you that your people will survive to see the sun rise the day after tomorrow. I cannot. All that I can guarantee you is that I will fight to the best of my ability, and that I will give my blood, my own life, to keep the city from falling, to keep the Xerxis from conquest, and to destroy Raptus."

Lord Romulus fell silent for a moment, glancing around at the grandmasters, these men and women who were normally so argumentative, so full of anger and suspicion.

"And now," he said, "I must ask all of you to do the same."

A rustle of grunts and whispers of surprise went through the chamber. Dust motes swirled in the daylight streaming down from the apex of the spire.

"Your acolytes and staff members have been deployed in

the manner the Voice has just described. Your combat mages have been assigned to work in squadrons, and many of them have been armed with weapons or armor of Malleum. Each squadron has been assigned one Wurm from Verlis's clan. They will be wearing bands of bright yellow around their arms to identify them to us. The squadrons will be spread around the city, with concentrations at the southern perimeter and around the Xerxis. Raptus seems to have been driven half mad by the power the Spawn of Wrath has given him. He is unlikely to attempt any sort of strategy, believing raw power to be enough. And with the level of magic he has achieved and his strength and the destructive capacity of his fire breath, he may be right.

"But that remains to be seen.

"The squadrons of combat mages and Wurm, and the acolytes placed on rooftops around Arcanum, have been tasked to destroy Raptus's raiders. To destroy Raptus himself, however, is the greater goal. He must be destroyed, or we have no hope. To do that will require the combined magic of the greatest mages in the entire world, the collective power of the Parliament of Mages.

"You, Grandmasters. Each and every one. The fate of our world rests in your hands. In our hands. Raptus has given us a chance to surrender. We have voted on the matter and the response was a resounding no. Let us deliver that response in person, and by force. While our guilds destroy his soldiers, we grandmasters must annihilate their general. We must prevail, or all is lost. And so I ask . . .

"Will you surrender ego and pride and submit your-selves to the command of the Voice and to my leadership in battle? Will you follow me, my friends? Will you stand with me until the last spell is cast?"

To Cassandra, it seemed that the entire chamber held its breath. Then Grandmaster Tarquine of the Caerleon Guild raised his fist high in a gesture of silent solidarity. To Cassandra's astonishment, Belladonna of the Strychnos imitated the gesture immediately. She was vindictive, cunning, and cruel, but her expression seemed quite genuine. Others followed suit. Parzival, the grim warrior who was the new Grandmaster of the Order of the Winter Star, sat just beside Cassandra, and as he raised his fist he glanced at her, a thin smile on his face. There was no amusement there, only resignation, and recognition of the wonder of this moment.

Cassandra raised her fist.

The Voice did the same.

When Verlis followed suit, no one found it odd.

They were united.

Timothy stood on the shore of the Island of Patience and stole a few moments of peace. The white sun gleamed down upon the hot sand and spread out across this strange parallel world, turning the sky a golden yellow that he missed terribly every moment he was away from here. The surf washed gently onto the shore, the wind rustling the long, drooping fronds of the Yaquis trees. He had climbed one of those trees upon his arrival here this morning, plucked a fruit, and eaten it before even beginning to descend.

The island had been his home for almost his entire life. Timothy had been born on Terra, his mother dying from trauma during the process, and when his father had realized how different he was—that he was a kind of puncture in the magical matrix, a blind spot in the world—Argus Cade had been so afraid of the world's reaction to his son that he opened a doorway into an alternate dimension and brought Timothy through. He had done this out of love and fear for his child. Argus had wanted to keep his son safe from the world. And in truth, Timothy had been happy growing up here with Ivar to teach and advise him, particularly after he built Sheridan as a playmate.

But he had wondered many times what his life would have been like if his father had dared keep him on Terra, had been brazen enough to raise him in Arcanum. Upon his father's death, when Leander had brought him to Arcanum, many had called him an abomination, assassins were sent to kill him, and even many of those who befriended him could not be trusted.

So much had changed in the little time since he had left Patience behind. At least on Terra.

On the island nothing had changed, and it filled his heart with pleasure to see it. He wished that he could simply stay here, that he could return to the simple happiness of his childhood. But he was not a child anymore, and back on Terra he had friends who needed him and many others who were also depending on him, much as it might trouble them. He had made promises, and if there was one thing that his father had taught him during his visits to the island, it was that promises must be kept.

Timothy stood on the jetty of rocks from which he had once fished and took a deep breath of ocean air. He stared out at the vast water before him, then hurled the pit of the Yaquis fruit out over the waves. Perhaps it would wash up on the shore of some other island, some other land, and a new Yaquis tree would grow. A seed from Patience, searching for roots in a strange new place.

He smiled grimly and turned, hurrying up the beach to the workshop where he had spent years designing and building his inventions. He had not even bothered to climb up to the treetop home where he and Ivar had lived. If he survived, he would return here and spend some time there.

Perhaps with Cassandra.

The thought quickened his pulse, as sweet to him as the fruit he had just tasted. Visiting Patience with Cassandra seemed the most obvious and perfect idea he had ever had.

But such thoughts would have to wait.

That morning he had been surprised to find the workshop dusty. One panel of the southern wall had been torn away, he presumed by one of the terrible storms that struck the island several times a year, and neither he nor Sheridan had been there to replace it. Rain had gotten in. Many of his plans and journals had been destroyed. Plants had grown wild around the entrance and up under the walls in places. Such things had been happening a little at a time, and during his previous return trips he had told himself he would take care of them the next time.

Now he wished he had done more to take care of the workshop, of the island, which had once been his whole life. The stolen moments out on the rocks had been an indulgence, but he knew that Raptus would not come to Arcanum until tomorrow morning, and this might be his last trip to Patience for some time. Or ever, though he didn't want to think about that.

Now, though, it was time for him to get back. In the workshop that day he had been busy. The Yaquis tree had its uses, but for his purposes he needed the branches and long hanging leaves of the Horax tree. Once he had used the stems of those leaves to make twine for fishing, but he had found other uses for it as well, weaving nets with which to capture some of the small animals on the island, and sometimes to dredge the shallows for black crabs. The twine, once woven, was nearly unbreakable. He had three perfect nets in the workshop and two others that needed repair.

But his time that day had been consumed by another task. Timothy was constantly sketching designs for inventions he might one day build, determined to perfect them before actually bringing them to life. Only since he had left Patience for the dangers of Terra had he even considered building weapons. But of late he had been designing a weapon that would fire projectiles, using Horax twine pulled taut and a shaft carved from a branch of that same tree. Horax wood was heavy and strong. It could be carved, but it was difficult to break. He thought that if whittled to a point and fired with enough speed, it would easily pierce the tough hide of a Wurm.

Timothy had built himself a crossbow.

Now he gathered the weapon, and a belt he had made with a pouch for the Horax shafts, and he started away from the workshop, out across the sand toward the magical door that stood on the beach. Once upon a time, only his father had ever come and gone through that door. But then Argus Cade had died and one day it had been Leander Maddox emerging from the other world, bringing the dreadful news.

At the door Timothy paused and took one last breath of the pure, sweet air of Patience. Then he went through.

On the other side of the door was a corridor on one of the upper floors of his father's house. From a window he could see all of Arcanum stretched out far below. Once there had been ghostfire lamps in the halls, but Timothy had replaced them with lanterns of hungry fire, nonmagical flame that would still burn if the glass was shattered. It was dangerous, but far better than ghostfire, which to him seemed so cruel.

He hurried down the corridor now, past the pipes that he had installed to carry water through his father's house without magic. His house. He still thought of it as his father's—sometimes even as the Cade estate, which was the way others referred to it. And yet perhaps that was all right. This beautiful old mansion with its dark wood and elegant tapestries was all that he had left to remind him of his father.

He had grown up on the island, but he was proud to call this house on August Hill his home.

As he rounded a corner, he heard the laughter of Wurm children, and the kind voice of Sheridan attempting to calm them. At the top of the long, circular stairs he looked down and saw several of the adult Wurm—the warriors of Verlis's clan—standing close, no doubt preparing to go out and join the squadrons to which they had been assigned.

He continued on until he reached the new workshop he had set up in the house when he had finally come to live here. Ivar was already inside. When Timothy entered, the Asura looked up calmly from Timothy's gyrocraft, the flying machine that the boy had built when he had first come to Arcanum and lived at SkyHaven.

"Good. You have returned," Ivar said. "I was worried."

"No need. I'm all right," Timothy replied. He laid the crossbow and the pouch of shafts on a table. "What do you think?"

The Asura picked up the weapon and examined it, testing the twine and the trigger. Ivar nodded thoughtfully. "It will work."

Timothy noticed that Ivar wore his knife, a long dagger with the markings of the Asura tribe. Ivar had not worn it for quite some time, and had been without it during his strange adventure to the south in pursuit of Grimshaw. The boy was both chilled and comforted to see it strapped to the Asura's hip again.

"What of the nets?" Ivar asked.

"Are you through with the repairs on the gyro?"

"Almost. I thought you would want to finish yourself, so you are certain it has all been done properly."

Timothy smiled. "I'm sure it has. But I'll look it over. Do you want to go back to Patience and pick up the nets?"

Ivar nodded. "I will be swift."

The boy thanked him, and then the Asura was gone. Timothy went over to the gyro and began to examine Ivar's work. His old friend was not an inventor the way that Timothy was, but he had no trouble understanding the mechanism of something once it was built. He had done an expert repair job.

There was a rap at the door.

Timothy turned to see Cassandra standing just inside the workroom. Her red hair seemed somehow darker to him, and wild, and the concern in her eyes gave her features a certain cast that made her seem more adult. She was not a child, of course, but she was still a girl, even though she was a grandmaster.

Yet there was little of the girl in her face just then.

"You didn't come to the Xerxis," she said, her voice oddly small.

Timothy found that his throat was dry, and he had to fight to force himself to speak. Just the sight of her did that to him. Darkly serious as she seemed, there was still a light in her eyes that no crisis could extinguish.

"I'm sorry," he said. "I . . . I did want to come to see you. But there was so much to do."

Cassandra stepped farther into the room. She wore robes of deep green that matched her eyes, with cuffs of gold that reminded him of the sky above Patience.

"We both have our responsibilities," she said. "But I have fulfilled mine for the moment. Until nightfall at least. Do you have a moment for me now?"

She was only inches away. Timothy reached out to take her hand.

"Of course."

Words failed him then.

But they were no longer necessary.

Edgar was perched on a small table in Timothy's bedroom, pecking at the remains of a fruit tart that the boy had never gotten around to finishing. Everyone was rushing about in preparation for Raptus's assault on the city, but he had nothing to do. When the time came—when sunrise brought the war to the outskirts of Arcanum—Edgar would be in the center of it all, at Timothy's side. But no one had asked his opinion on the deployment of combat mages or the best way to assault Wurm from the air, so in the midst of all the franticness and fear, he was left to his own devices.

He hated it.

Not the fruit tart. Though it had gone a bit stale. No, Edgar hated being surrounded by such anxiety and determination and feeling so useless. It felt as though tiny insects were creeping underneath his feathers. He was constantly ruffling them and hopping about, unable to settle down.

From out in the hallway there came a noise, the clank of wood on metal. Edgar tilted his head and paused to listen more closely. When he heard the familiar toot of steam escaping from the valve on the side of Sheridan's head, a kind of relief went through him. Ever since Timothy had left the island and come to live in Arcanum, the rook and the mechanical man had been friends. They often bickered, and Edgar found that sometimes he could not stop himself from making wry comments, but Sheridan never seemed to mind.

The fruit tart entirely forgotten, he hopped off the table and spread his wings, flying to the door. He did not fly out into the corridor right away, however. Now that the Wurm children had at last given up tormenting him, he did not want to draw their attention again, so he landed on the floor and peeked out into the hall. Sheridan was alone, carrying a tea tray.

Edgar hopped into the hall and took flight.

"Good afternoon, Sheridan," the rook said.

With a whir of gears the mechanical man's head spun all the way around. "Oh, hello, Edgar."

The rook alighted on Sheridan's shoulder. "Actually, I take it back. Nothing good about today, is there?"

Sheridan turned his head around to look where he was going. Another hiss of steam escaped his head. "Every day we're alive is a good day. That's what I think."

Edgar ruffled his feathers, then folded his wings tightly against his back. He scratched at his chest with his beak. "Forever the optimist. All right, I'm with you. If we're still alive at this time tomorrow, I'll think it's a heck of a day."

"You must have faith, Edgar," the mechanical man chided, carrying the tray down the corridor toward Timothy's home workshop.

"I'd better. I'm going to be out there fighting the Wurm tomorrow."

Sheridan sighed. "I wish I were going to be with you. I have no taste for war, but I hate the idea of staying behind and waiting for news."

Edgar tilted his head. "You're doing your part, pal. Those Wurm kids get on my nerves, but their parents need someone to look out for them."

"I still believe they ought to have left with the mage children," Sheridan said. "If the attackers should get as far as August Hill—"

"We'll have to hope the magical defenses Argus built into this place will protect them. But Verlis and Cythra didn't want to send them off with just mages to look out for them. If the kids got too rambunctious, there could be trouble."

Sheridan shook his head. "Still, there is no trust. They have to fight side by side for the lives of us all, but they dare not turn their backs on one another."

"Maybe someday," Edgar said. "But someday's a ways off still."

They reached the workshop and found the door open several inches. Sheridan balanced the tray in one hand and pushed it open the rest of the way.

"Good afternoon, Timothy. You've been working so hard, I thought you might like—"

Edgar blinked several times, his beak open in surprise. Timothy and Cassandra stood in the middle of the workshop in a tight embrace, lost in a passionate kiss. As Sheridan spoke up, they broke apart.

"Sheridan!" the boy said, face flushed scarlet. He stammered something and then looked over at the girl.

For her part Cassandra only smiled shyly and gave a soft laugh. That seemed to set Timothy at ease.

"You've caught us by surprise, I'm afraid," Timothy said.

"And you, us," Sheridan replied.

"Way to go, Tim," Edgar said, prompting another blush of embarrassment from the boy and another laugh from Cassandra. "We're proud of you."

Edgar truly was pleased. He had seen the affection developing between the two young ones for quite some time, and with the shadow of the war looming, they had brought a spark of light and life into a dark time. He hoped they knew how fortunate they were to have found that spark.

"Sheridan," the rook said, "leave the tray. Let the kids get back to what they were doing before we interrupted."

The mechanical man gave a loud toot of steam and then set the tea tray on a worktable. "Yes, of course. Terribly sorry. Let me know if you need anything else."

Edgar laughed and shifted position on Sheridan's shoulder, talons scratching metal. "They're not going to need anything. That tea's gonna sit there and get cold too, I'd wager."

As Sheridan left the room, pulling the door behind them, Edgar glanced back and saw Tim and Cassandra holding hands and smiling at each other, still a bit shy.

Right there, Edgar thought. *That's what we're fighting for.*

CHAPTER TEN

When the first light of dawn touched the tips of the spires of Arcanum the following morning—the day of the war—Carlyle was stationed at the southern perimeter of the city. He had been placed in command of the squadron that consisted of the combat mages of the Order of Alhazred and the Strychnos guild. He was at first reluctant to agree to this pairing. The mages of the Strychnos were female and nearly all statuesque and elegant. He had worried that for some of the Alhazred mages, the Strychnos would be too great a distraction. But he needn't have been concerned. They were beautiful, but they were cold, specializing in plants and poison. They were gravely serious.

He had also underestimated his own combat mages. Today they were all equally serious. Nothing would distract them from the task at hand.

Other squadrons had been put into place around the city. From his vantage point, Carlyle could only see those nearest to him to the east and west. Though they had been broken up by guild—best to keep together those mages used to working as a team—no one carried a banner trumpeting their allegiance. They all shared one allegiance today.

The southern perimeter of the city was mostly small shops and offices, as well as apartment buildings where many of the less skilled mages worked. Magical laborers and support staff could not afford more luxurious homes. It was troubling, because they could also least afford to lose the homes they had, and Carlyle could not see how it was possible that most of the buildings around him would not be reduced to rubble by the coming battle.

With the sunrise the mages in his squadron set themselves into a battle stance, ready for an attack at any moment. Many of them crackled with pent-up magic, the light of various spells flickering from their eyes and sparking from their fingertips.

Carlyle watched the southern horizon with growing unease. Cythra was the Wurm assigned to their squadron, and Carlyle had sent her south as a scout so that she could return and give them advance warning of Raptus's arrival. The sight of anything larger than a bird in the lightening sky would signal the beginning of war, and he knew that many of those around him would not survive it. There would be bloodshed. And some of that blood might be his own.

Yet he was prepared for that. He had served as a combat

mage, and faithfully as an aide to the Grandmaster of the Order of Alhazred. If he died defending this city and all of mage civilization, that was an honorable death.

Still, he said a prayer to the gods—for his own sake and that of so many others—that it would not come to that.

"Commander Carlyle!" shouted a voice.

He spun to see Nimue, one of the best combat mages in the ranks of the Order of Alhazred, hurrying through the squadron toward him. Like many others, she had not worked daily at SkyHaven but instead had been working in Arcanum, both as a scholar at the University of Saint Germain and as a spy. When the late Grandmaster Maddox had reviewed all the mages who were members of the order, he had dismissed those with ties too close to Nicodemus, knowing they were likely to be treacherous. But Leander and Carlyle had both agreed Nimue was beyond reproach and utterly loyal to the order, not to any one individual who might become grandmaster. He was relieved to have her as part of his squadron.

"Nimue," he said as she approached.

Some of the Strychnos mages and several of the Alhazred gathered nearer to hear what she had to report. Carlyle rounded on them.

"Vigilance, all of you! Be taken off guard, and it will cost us all!"

Nimue nodded in grim approval. Had she been commanding the squadron, she would have reacted the same way. Her long white-blond hair was tied back tightly to keep it out of her face, and her ice blue eyes were severe. Magical power radiated from within her, but not with the kind of obvious display some of the other mages put on.

"What news?" Carlyle asked.

"Caiaphas, whom you have charged with organizing our acolytes, has asked me to inform you that they are all in place at the top of the Wandsworth Bank Building."

Carlyle nodded and turned to gaze northward toward the center of Arcanum. Wandsworth Bank was perhaps half a mile away and a dozen stories high. It was a hut in comparison to the spires in the city center, but one of the taller buildings out here on the outskirts. Each of the guilds had gathered all of the magical weaponry they could find. Some had spell-bombs that would explode on contact and burn their targets or transform them into mud toads or something equally offensive. Others had enchanted blades that would cut whatever they touched. Most common, however, were curse-cannons, because they had been simple enough for the guilds to create hundreds of them just in the past day. They were little more than hollow shafts of wood loaded with powerful curse attacks that could be shot at a target by a simple snap of the wrist. They could only be used once each, but a blast from a curse-cannon ought to at least wound the Wurm that it struck. If an acolyte's aim was good enough and they struck something vital, they might even be able to kill with one shot.

After those weapons ran out, they would be left with only whatever edged weapons they had brought with them and their own magical skills. But acolytes were not combat mages. Most Wurm had skill and power with magic that was nearly as significant as that of an acolyte, and the Wurm were physically stronger, far more vicious . . . and they had their fire.

If the war was still raging when they ran out of the weapons that had been supplied to them, the acolytes up on those rooftops would be easy prey. But they did not lack for courage. They would fight for Arcanum. For Terra.

"It's hard, isn't it?" Nimue asked, her voice quiet so she would not be overheard.

Carlyle frowned. "How do you mean?"

Her ice blue eyes narrowed. "It should never have come to this. The Parliament betrayed the Wurm before my mother was born. What they did was wrong. If they'd just let the Wurm live in Tora'nah in peace, all those years ago . . ." She scowled in disgust.

Carlyle nodded. "They were the villains back then. It was treachery of the worst kind. But now Raptus wants to destroy our entire civilization. He's already slaughtered hundreds, perhaps thousands, on his way here, many of them children and noncombatants. Whatever was done to his people in that dark time, there must be a better path to the future than this. I wish what happened then had not happened, but I won't stand by while he blazes his trail of vengeance. My friends and family were not responsible for what happened to his people. My children did nothing wrong."

Nimue stared at him for a long time. "I wasn't aware you had children."

"They live with their mother in Torwall."

She let out a long breath and then turned so that she stood beside him, the two of them looking at the southern horizon along with the rest of the squadron.

"Still, it didn't have to be like this," she said after a moment.

"No," Carlyle agreed. "It didn't."

Even as he spoke the words, voices were raised in alarm, and the squadron began to move. Carlyle shouted orders.

A single Wurm had been spotted coming toward the city, silhouetted against the sky in the early-morning sunlight. It was Cythra, arm bands whipping behind her as she flew. Her speed was incredible.

A moment later Carlyle understood why she was flying so fast. One by one, other Wurm began to appear in the southern sky. First only a few, but then several dozen, and then several dozen more. He lost count fairly quickly. There must have been two or three hundred, all told.

He felt the magic crackling around his fingers, ready for war.

Then the ground shook, just slightly, beneath his feet. On the horizon were the country homes of some mages who preferred not to live in the city and then, beyond those, nothing but forest and the road going south.

Trees cracked and fell, knocked aside as Raptus stepped from the forest, so large that it looked doubtful his wings could hold him up. As tall as the tallest tree. Even taller. There were spires in Arcanum that did not reach his height.

"By all the gods of old," Carlyle whispered.

"After seeing that," Nimue rasped beside him, "how can you still believe in gods?"

Magic swirled in the open palm of Alethea Borgia, the Voice of Parliament. She stood in the courtyard before the main entrance of the Xerxis, surrounded by the gathered grandmasters of every guild. Shifting in that magic was a figure made of mist and shades of green, the image of one of the acolytes who worked for the Voice up in the watchtower, the secret chamber in the Xerxis from which every corner of Arcanum could be magically viewed.

"Speak quickly," the Voice demanded of the woman whose image shifted on her palm. "Do any of the watchtower spyglasses show Wurm approaching the city from any other direction?"

The rest of the grandmasters were just as silent as if Alethea had stolen their voices.

"No, Madame Voice," the sentinel of the watchtower reported. "They come only from the south. But . . . if you could see Raptus . . ."

There was fear in that voice. Cassandra heard it, and she glanced at some of the grandmasters gathered around her. Foxheart twisted his upper lip in disdain. Bayonnis of the Celestial Guild swallowed visibly and glanced about as though wishing for a clear path along which to flee. Tarquine of the

Caerleon and Parzival of the Winter Star stood together, and it was clear that they knew and trusted each other. They might even have been friends, although such allegiances had long been considered risky within Parliament. The two mages exchanged a grim look at the tone of the sentinel's voice.

"We shall see him," the Voice assured her, and as such, assured them all. "And soon."

Lord Romulus had been clutching his massive black helmet beneath his arm, offering a rare glimpse of his face. His grim features seemed sculpted from stone and his eyes burned with the intensity of hungry fire. He stood a foot and a half taller than any other member of their congregation, so attention was always on him. This morning more than ever.

At the Voice's words, Romulus raised his helmet up by one of its horns and shook it in the air. "That's it, then. We're off! And remember, brothers and sisters, we do not have room for half measures. If we fall, so falls Arcanum, and all of Terra behind her."

He began barking orders as he slipped the helmet down to hide his face again, leaving only those gleaming, brutal eyes revealed. Then he was running, gesturing as he did so, reminding grandmasters what their positions were to be, commanding even the greatest among them as though he had been born to it. And Cassandra thought perhaps he had. Lord Romulus had been Timothy's enemy for so long that it had taken her time to realize that they were fortunate now to be on his side.

The bells were ringing all through the city, warning of the attack of the Wurm. The gathered grandmasters ran for the collection of sky carriages that had been awaiting them. Some got inside, but most of them climbed on top of the crafts or stood on the metal bars that ran around the outside, holding on to handles that were put in place for servants and footmen. Cassandra thought these archmages had probably never imagined themselves riding sky carriages the way their lowliest servants might, but this was a time of change and an age of firsts.

They needed to be ready as they rode through the sky, prepared for an aerial assault, positioned to cast spells and hurl devastating curses should the Wurm fall on them while they were still in flight. Yet such things were the least of their concerns. Turning away these attacks would be simple enough for the mages. It was Raptus that concerned them. He was their one and only target. The various facets of the war had been assigned to others. Raptus was theirs.

Cassandra held on to the back of a sky carriage and tried to keep her footing, thinking how ridiculous and embarrassing it would be if she fell off. She felt painfully out of place among archmages of legendary status and power. As the granddaughter of Nicodemus, she was innately stronger with magic than the average mage, and she had worked all her life to master the skills necessary to wield such power, to tap deeply into the magical matrix. But alongside such men and women, she felt herself a novice.

But she would say nothing. As grandmaster of her order

she had been called to duty this day, and if that duty cost her her life, then so be it.

The thirteen sky carriages raced along, perhaps fifty feet above the ground. The grandmasters were silent and grim, except for Parzival of the Winter Star, who caught Cassandra's eye and smiled. It was not a flirtatious smile, but one of encouragement, as if to say he had faith in her. Though she was sure he could not know her well enough to have such confidence, still she smiled in return, grateful.

The bells seemed to grow louder. Cassandra looked all around, scanning the upper floors of some of the taller buildings. She knew that the buildings where the acolytes had been stationed were bespelled with magic that made them nearly fireproof, but still they all seemed like towering, hollow tombs to her. As they passed, many of the acolytes came to lean off roofs and cheer them, these archmages going to war. The best of the best. Cassandra gnawed her lip each time she saw the mages urging them forward with such passion.

So many of them would soon be dead.

She wished that she was on one of the lead carriages with Romulus and the Voice. They knew, at least, whereas to so many of those around her she was a total stranger. Cassandra did not want to die among strangers.

"There!" shouted Belladonna from the sky carriage beside hers.

Cassandra looked up and saw that the Wurm invasion had already reached farther into the city than she had thought.

The dragonkin were dark against the morning sky, most clad in crimson or black armor, their wings like blades slashing the air. They were not far ahead and several had obviously seen the caravan of sky carriages and now began to dip their wings, preparing for an attack.

A pair of acolytes appeared on the roof of a library up ahead. They hurled spell-bombs at the three Wurm. One of them was enveloped in a cloud of icy mist, and when it emerged from that cloud it was crusted with frost, nearly frozen solid. The Wurm fell, left wing striking the library and shattering like glass. It broke into shards when it hit the ground. The other spell-bomb was explosive, and it went off with such concussive force that it sent the other two Wurm careening through the air. One of them struck a Spiral Guild assembly hall and fell unconscious. The other caught a corner of a building and held on. When it looked up, its eyes blazed with fresh hatred.

They weren't easy to kill.

Several others had seen the conflict brewing and now flew in from east and west, peeling away from the northward course so many others were following—and there were dozens of them now, hordes of Wurm moving across the city.

A curse-cannon fired, the sound like a resonant hand clap, and Cassandra saw the magic had blown a Wurm out of the sky.

A cadre of five Wurm warriors descended upon the roof of the library with swords and axes, breathing the fire of their ancestors from the furnaces in their gullets. The acolytes on the library were slaughtered. Cassandra heard their shouts of pain and anguish and fury.

Her knuckles were white from the way she gripped the handle on the outside of that sky carriage. The wind whipped her hair back, and she gritted her teeth against it as the carriage picked up speed. Her skin prickled with the magic that seethed inside her, the force ready to be unleashed. Those acolytes had drawn the focus away from the grandmasters and died as a result. But they had also done one other thing. They had shown that the Wurm were not as difficult to kill as Parliament had feared. If she calculated all the acolytes and combat mages, the odds were perhaps one hundred to one, mages versus Wurm. The invaders had no chance of winning. It was a matter of attrition.

Or it would have been, if not for Raptus.

And now the sky carriages turned into a broad avenue headed due south, and she saw him for the first time. Even over the tops of several residential buildings, she could see his massive, horned head and the spread of his wings, which seemed to throw a shadow over an entire block of Arcanum. Primal terror—something dredged up through memories passed down from her ancestors—filled her. But Cassandra refused to allow it to take hold.

The sky carriages began to spread out to prevent themselves from being attacked all at once. Then they rounded another corner and saw the ruin of the south side of Arcanum. Buildings had been razed to the ground and were now nothing but burning rubble. From every visible shelter, combat mages tried valiantly to slow Raptus's march across the city. There were Wurm raiders flying high above, but the combat mages on the ground ignored them now, leaving them for the city's other defenders, and likewise the Wurm ignored the mages on the ground. Why bother with them, when Raptus was coming?

The gigantic Wurm seemed as tall to her as the spire of the Xerxis. He loomed above the ruin, magic crackling and dancing all over his leathery flesh. His wings were partially spread and his talons held out in front of him as though he might try to lunge at them. Yet when the thirteen sky carriages carrying the entire Parliament of Mages appeared, one by one, at the front line of the war where hundreds had already died, Raptus seemed barely to notice.

Those huge eyes opened wide, gleaming a sickly yellow, and gouts of fire blazed from his snout. A ragtag collection of combat mages stood their ground at his feet, staring up at the hundred-foot-tall monster. They ought to have been beneath his notice, but this handful of combat mages had survived his onslaught. Even now magic of many colors coalesced around their upraised fists, and they began to shout in unison—joined in battle as their individual guilds had never been joined—and the magic was about to leap from them.

Raptus opened his great maw and Cassandra felt the suction of his inhalation tugging at her, shaking the sky carriage in which she rode.

"Defend yourselves!" Tarquine shouted, shooting a glance at Parzival and then at Cassandra.

The grandmasters threw up defensive magic shields in the same instant that the volcanic fire erupted from the massive jaws of Raptus. It was like a hurricane of flame, blasting out across the rubble of the entire block. The flames buffeted the grandmasters' shields but were turned away easily.

As for the handful of combat mages who had been on the ground and up close to Raptus . . . they were gone. Incinerated completely. Their magics had helped to slow the monstrous Wurm's assault, and they had survived longer than any of their comrades, but that was over now.

One of the dead was Carlyle.

Cassandra had seen him at the last moment, before the fire was battering the shimmering shield of golden energy she had manifested from her open hands, and in the noise and fury of the moment, she could not even scream. Grief clutched her heart, but she fought against it as if it were its own war.

Teeth gritted tightly, she began to shout a kind of battle cry, surprising even herself. The others took up the cry and the sky carriage cruised to a halt.

They all leaped off and began to run across burning cobblestones and blasted earth. From the ruins all around, combat mages who had been fighting in other parts of the southern perimeter rushed to join them. The line of grandmasters and combat mages ranged along several blocks in a rough half circle, and all of them began to attack Raptus. Magic struck him like a thunderous storm hammer, stabbed him with lightning, filled his eyes and mouth and lungs with poison.

Raptus began to laugh, the noise echoing out over Arcanum, drowning out even the warning bells.

"Now it becomes interesting," the Wurm said, still laughing. "I want you all to remember later, if any of you survive, that you had a chance to surrender and refused. That you brought the fire down upon yourselves."

And he laughed. Then his wings spread, magic leaping from him in destructive bolts, Raptus inhaled again, the fire churning in him, ready to burn everything in his path.

Timothy had gotten up before dawn and prepared the gyrocraft. While it was still full dark and the morning was not even a glimmer on the horizon, he and Ivar had set off from a balcony at the rear of his father's house and flown west from August Hill. Edgar had hesitated, seemingly reluctant to leave Sheridan behind, but the rook knew that someone had to watch over the Wurm children and eventually Sheridan had demanded they depart. When Timothy had piloted the gyro away from the house, Edgar had been flying beside him, leaving the big mansion empty save for the mechanical man and his young charges.

It had taken some hard work, but Timothy had rigged the gyro so that he could steer with pedals at his feet, leaving his hands mostly free. Ivar would have to do most of the aerial fighting, with the nets Timothy had made and a set of throwing knives Lord Romulus had given him. The plan was for them to swing in behind the Wurm raiders who had already crossed the city line and begun to attack with fire and sorcery. Neither of them was under any illusions. They were well aware that there was a limit to how effective they could be in the air, and that as soon as they had run out of weapons they would have to land. Timothy planned to fly the gyro to the nearest rooftop battle, where they'd abandon the invention and fight hand to hand. Ivar had his tribal dagger and Timothy had the sword he had gotten from the Legion Nocturne at the battle of Twilight.

But first, the air.

He had remained airborne just east of Arcanum and awaited sunrise. When he heard the bells begin to ring in the distance, shortly after dawn, he had begun to fly toward the perimeter of the city, sneaking around behind the invading army. Now he saw several Wurm in the sky. Beyond them, he saw Raptus.

"Look at him," he whispered.

"The monster is even larger," Ivar said.

"At least twice as big as he was before." Timothy swallowed, his throat dry and sore, and he picked up the crossbow he'd made. He snatched up a sharpened wooden shaft and nocked it into place, working the controls of the gyro with his feet. "But Raptus isn't our target. The grandmasters are going to take care of him. They'll be all right. The combined magic of all of those archmages . . . they'll be fine."

He wished he could believe his own words, but they sounded hollow even to him. On the other hand, what could he do? One boy without any magical ability at all against a hundred-foot-tall dragon? Nothing. He could do nothing against Raptus. Timothy had considered what might happen if he touched the gigantic Wurm—with the magic of the Spawn of Wrath coursing through him—but he could not imagine Raptus allowing him to get close enough to do so. He would be incinerated.

No, the mages would handle him.

Edgar had been flying above them, surveying the battle from on high. Now the rook swooped lower, cawing loudly. "All right, Tim. The war's on. Raptus's soldiers are completely focused on what's in front of them."

"Let's get them," Timothy said, and he worked the left pedal and turned them to pursue the nearest Wurm. His plan had worked perfectly, bringing them in behind the Wurm raiders. The Wurm were not flying at anywhere near their top speed, taking their time surveying the city below to watch for an attack.

Timothy increased the gyro's speed and began to gain on the beast. Edgar flew as quickly as he could, a black blur beside him, but made not a sound.

Farther ahead he saw members of Verlis's clan take flight from hidden places on rooftops and spires. Off to the east a pair of Wurm began to tear into each other in midair, fire spilling down from both of them, magic sparking where their claws struck. Chaos erupted. The bells still rang across Arcanum. From a city square down below, a squadron of combat mages began to cast spells skyward.

Timothy kept to the outer edge of the battle and doggedly pursued the Wurm nearest him. In moments he had pulled up near enough to draw its attention. The boy signaled to Edgar. The rook winked at him and then flew directly across the Wurm's path, so close that the Wurm's breath must have warmed him. Then Edgar circled around and back toward Timothy. The Wurm twisted its head to look back over its wings, and its yellow eyes narrowed in surprise and anger when it spotted the gyrocraft.

With a press of a pedal, Timothy veered west. The Wurm dipped its left wing and turned to follow. Which was precisely what Timothy had wanted.

"Have you got him?" he called back to Ivar.

"Slow down," the Asura replied, his voice curt. "Let him get confident."

Timothy glanced back to see the Wurm chasing after them, fire streaming from its nostrils and the corners of its mouth, jaws gnashing. It was thirty feet away, then twenty, gaining fast. It opened its maw, and Timothy could see the fire churning down inside its throat.

"It's going to—" the boy began.

Edgar came down at blinding speed, cutting across in front of the Wurm again, but this time with his talons out. He tore at the invader's face, distracting it further.

Ivar threw a knife. It sliced through the air and went into the Wurm's open mouth. The beast flinched backward with a cry of pain, and when it shook itself to try to get rid of the blade, it turned its head and Timothy could see the point of the blade sticking out the back of its neck.

The Wurm reached up to try to pull the blade out of its mouth—blood spilling from its jaws now in place of flame—and Ivar took that moment to act. The gyrocraft had been redesigned so that he and Timothy were back to back, Ivar facing what was behind them, and his seat was open to the sky on top. Now he stood and hurled one of the nets onto the Wurm. Its wings and arms became immediately tangled, and as it struggled, it weakened from its wound and loss of blood. A blast of fire came out of its maw and burned a hole in the net, but still it was tangled, and it began to fall.

"Way to go!" Timothy shouted.

He heard a loud cawing and then Edgar calling his name in alarm. But even as he heard the warning he saw something moving out of the corner of his eye. It was above him and to the left, and he turned the gyro toward it. A Wurm raider was bearing down on them. He and Ivar shouted warnings to each other in the same moment. Timothy raised his crossbow and fired, the gyrocraft's propeller whirring above him.

The crossbow shaft struck the Wurm in the eye, killing it instantly.

"That was close," Edgar called, flying beside him.

Timothy's heart was beating so hard he could barely respond. He veered the gyro around and headed west for several seconds to get some distance from the battle, then turned around. The Wurm raiders were all over the southern end of the city now, gathering in clusters to attack the buildings from which the acolytes were launching magical assaults and firing curse-cannons. Timothy had planned to follow his strategy a second time, like a prowling jungle cat, cutting the strays away from the edges of the herd. He would fly in again and lure a Wurm or two after the gyro.

A massive flash of silver light like liquid metal exploded in the midst of a south Arcanum neighborhood. Timothy raised a hand to shield his eyes from the burst of brilliance, and then narrowed his eyes, trying to see what had caused it. As the silver magic dissipated, showering down like rain on the ruin of an entire city block, Timothy saw that Raptus was down.

The monstrous Wurm—not really a Wurm anymore, but the biggest dragon who'd ever walked the soil of Terra— was on his side on the ground, one wing crumpled beneath him. Sparks of silver magic flickered all over him, mixing with the dark sorcery that emanated from within Raptus. But more than sparks. On the leathery flesh of his upper torso was a place where his skin had turned that same silver color.

It began to run, the silver spreading on his flesh. Raptus roared.

In a vast semicircle around him, the grandmasters began to move in for the kill as the spell they had all worked to cast together did its damage, poisoning Raptus with a magic that Timothy knew would seep into him, find his heart, and kill him. That had been Lord Romulus's plan, and it seemed to be—

Timothy could not finish the thought.

Raptus roared again and spread his wings wide, beating them with enough force that many of the grandmasters were thrown from their feet. The gigantic dragon pushed himself up, all one hundred feet of him, and stood. With a rage like nothing Timothy had ever seen, eyes blind with fury, Raptus tore at his chest, digging furrows in flesh and silver poison alike.

Then he lowered his massive head and snarled, and the magic enveloping him shimmered and grew brighter by far, and the silver that had been crawling over his flesh began to peel off and fall like metallic snow. Raptus shook himself once, gave another beat of his wings, and it was all gone.

The Parliament's plan had failed.

Timothy thought back to Twilight, to the moment when he had realized that they had no chance at victory, that they were going to lose.

This felt very much like that.

A chill passed through him as he realized that he knew a way to beat Raptus. Maybe the only way. And yet he knew that the price of victory might be nearly as terrible as defeat.

CHAPTER ELEVEN

Some of the grandmasters were shouting in triumph. Foxheart even called a hearty congratulations across the rubble of a school to Lord Romulus. But Cassandra noticed that the Grandmaster of the Legion Nocturne did not respond. He was still in combat stance, body low and legs tensed to attack, magic churning around his clenched fists as he watched Raptus reeling from the effects of the poisonous curse that the grandmasters had combined all of their magics to cast. The silver was spreading like fungus across the gigantic Wurm's body.

And then it wasn't.

Raptus shook, as though he were having some sort of seizure, and Cassandra felt the ground tremble under her feet. Then the gigantic beast began to stand. Even half-crouched, he towered over the grandmasters. She brought her hands up, summoning a combat spell that would shatter the bones of a mage and aiming for Raptus's eyes.

Then the monstrosity flapped his wings and the wind struck her, tearing her off the ground and hurling her through the air.

Cassandra struck the ground in an open courtyard that had once held an elegant fountain. It was shattered and the water sprayed aimlessly across cracked cobblestones. She hit the ground and rolled, banging elbows and one shoulder hard enough that after she came to rest she had to lay there a moment to determine that nothing was broken. Cold water from the broken fountain pooled beneath her, soaking through her robes.

"Up!" someone shouted. "Get up! We cannot let the monster recover!"

Dazed, she forced herself to respond. Her ears were ringing, and she realized that she had struck her head on the cobblestones as well. Cassandra rose and looked around. So many faces that she barely recognized, their names a jumble to her. There were combat mages mixed in with the grandmasters now, their battle plan falling apart. But she saw the Voice and Foxheart and Arcturus Tot and so she began to head toward them.

Then all the mages and archmages around her were running, and she found herself falling into step beside them. She cursed, shaking her head to clear it.

"Cassandra, are you all right?" called a voice.

She turned and saw Tarquine and Parzival off to her left.

Belladonna of the Strychnos was with them, and she recognized Aloysius of the Spiral Guild as well, an old man who seemed even more ancient in that moment, face blanched with terror. But none of them were looking at her and she had no idea which of them had called her name.

Then she heard another voice shouting up ahead, a familiar, rumbling bass. Over the heads of grandmasters and combat mages who were renewing their assault on Raptus, she saw one who stood head and shoulders above all the others. Lord Romulus still wore his horned helmet and the heavy robes of the Legion Nocturne, and his very presence, his seeming indestructibility, made him even more of a rallying point than any command he might shout. The sight of him, blue light springing from his hands, was enough to help clear Cassandra's head.

She charged toward Romulus.

Beyond him, Raptus roared again and spread his wings. For the first time she noticed that there was no sign of the silver poison on his flesh. Her stomach gave a sickening twist as she realized that Raptus was completely unharmed. The entire Parliament had combined their power to cast that spell, and the Wurm had only been staggered a few moments before his own magic had burned off the curse.

We should have used a combat spell, not poison, she thought wildly. *Should have tried to just blast a hole right through him!*

But from what Romulus had told them about the way Raptus had healed after such attacks during the battle of Twilight, they had all agreed that the monster's hide was too tough, and that the magic that seemed to suffuse his entire body would just heal him.

What now?

Cassandra glanced around for cover. They should all be falling back, she realized, withdrawing from the burning rubble to the next block. But Romulus wasn't ready for a strategic withdrawal yet; he was shouting at the combat mages and grandmasters, ordering them to spread out again and prepare for another attack.

But Raptus wasn't going to give them that much time.

Many of the grandmasters continued their attack as they raced to follow Romulus's instructions. Bayonnis of the Celestial Guild opened his mouth and, almost as though he were a Wurm, black fire erupted and seared the air. It struck Raptus's left wing and stuck there, burning the flesh like acid. The Hecate Grandmaster, a woman whose name Cassandra could not recall, raised her hands—fingertips as black as those of a Nimib assassin—and purple-black magic crackled from them, striking the gigantic Wurm in the lower torso. The attack was harmlessly absorbed.

Fool, Cassandra thought. Dark magic was not going to affect a beast such as Raptus.

She had to get to Romulus, convince him to command them all to find cover and attack from there. Parts of the city were going to have to be sacrificed. Hard decisions had to be made. If the Wurm raiders could all be destroyed—and she had no doubt that they would be—then every mage in Arcanum could converge on Raptus.

Every surviving mage, at least.

From off to her left, someone cast a spell that struck Raptus in the face with a flash like lightning. Ice formed on his horns and covered his eyes, and steam rose from his great maw. But Raptus only shook, cracking the ice, and more steam rose as it melted away.

There were dozens of people all around her, grand-masters and combat mages both, and she shoved past a woman she didn't recognize, and a man that she did only vaguely. With a sideways glance she saw Tarquine and Parzival, and from the motion of his arms and the disappointment on his face, she realized that the ice spell had come from Parzival. Again she felt a twist inside her. If the Grandmaster of the Order of the Winter Star could not use an ice spell on Raptus, that was another type of magic they could forget about even trying again.

They were running out of options.

Raptus spread his wings again. Cassandra stopped running and dropped into a crouch, throwing up a magical shield. She had been fortunate not to brake any bones after being blown across the cobblestones and rubble the first time.

But Raptus was not trying to blow them back. He did not even flap his wings. Instead he darted his head down at them like a serpent ready to bite. His jaws opened wide. Cassandra saw the rows of long, thin fangs, each as tall as she was.

Then the liquid flame shot from his burning maw, a tidal

wave of fire that engulfed the entire left side of their crescent attack. Cassandra screamed and threw herself back as the fire roared and splashed only twenty or thirty feet away from her. The heat seared her flesh and singed her hair. Smoke rose up from her robes as she stared in horror, watching all those mages being buried beneath that volcanic blast.

"No!" she cried, throat raw from the heat.

She tried to remember who she had seen over there. Aloysius, certainly. Tarquine and . . .

The lake of fire began to dissipate. There had been dozens of men and women there, combat mages and grandmasters alike. Now there were four, each of them encased in a shimmering golden sheath of magic. Only those four had erected defenses in time and been powerful enough to withstand Raptus's fire.

Of the four, she recognized only Tarquine of the Caerleon. She put a hand over her mouth in horror as she saw him look around for Parzival, saw the look in his eyes as he realized his friend was dead. And yet Parzival had been only one of so many. Aloysius of the Spiral Guild. Bayonnis of the Celestial Guild. Mistress Belladonna, Grandmaster of the Strychnos, and for so long filled with hate for Timothy Cade.

All dead.

And so many more.

Cassandra forced herself to push her fear aside, and she reached down deep within herself, deeper still, tapping into the magical matrix from which they all drew. She dredged something up from the depths of the matrix, magic like nothing she had ever dared try to wield. Her body thrummed with it, her hair crackling with static, and white light of such purity as she had never imagined burst into illumination around her hands.

She cried out to the three moons as though they might hear her, and she punched the sky, letting her rage carry that pure white magic. It shot from her hands, chilling the air as it passed, snuffing the flames beneath it. The spell struck Raptus in the left shoulder and the crack of bone could be heard echoing all across the remains of southern Arcanum.

Sickly yellow eyes wide, the hundred-foot Wurm looked down at his shoulder in astonishment at the pain. He had been injured.

A sudden tumult of voices rose, then, mages shouting in triumph. Despite the death of so many, they redoubled their efforts. Spell after spell painted the sky, striking Raptus, most of them doing nothing. Again liquid fire dripped from the corners of his jaws, showering down to the ground like lava slipping over the edges of a volcano mouth.

He could be hurt. Cassandra was glad of that. But her assault had caused the others to do the opposite of what she knew they ought to be doing. Lord Romulus shouted again, and now he was running at Raptus as though he could attack the Wurm directly, hand to hand.

"No," she whispered, unable to hear her own voice amid the cacophony of battle.

It had felt good, hurting Raptus. But they could not defeat him. Not this way. His magic deflected most attacks and healed others, and his fire would soon raze the entire city to the ground. The Xerxis would be nothing but embers soon.

Cassandra looked around her at what remained of the most powerful mages in the world. Some were already dead. The rest would soon join them. A great weight of sadness descended upon her as she realized that she, too, would die before the morning was out.

Tears slipped down her cheeks as she raised her hands, summoning another spell, mustering as much destructive force as she could manage. Then she ran to join the others in battle.

To join them in death.

Ivar held on to the sides of the gyrocraft and hoped that Timothy wasn't pushing the invention beyond its capacity. They were diving toward the ground at such a hard angle that Ivar was looking almost straight up at the sky. He forced himself to twist sideways so that he could get a look at their destination.

Raptus was under attack. The grandmasters and combat mages who still lived were circling around the monster. Instead of another unified assault, however, they were casting magic with wild abandon, one spell after another. The cumulative effect of the attacks could not be great, but they were at least keeping Raptus distracted for a moment. None of those spells was going to kill the beast, but for the moment they were annoying enough to have stopped his advance into the city. Soon, though, the furnace in Raptus's chest would replenish his natural flame, and he would let loose another fiery attack on his enemies.

And then it would be over. All that would remain would be for Raptus to complete his destruction of Arcanum, after which the Wurm would begin their march across the entire planet of Terra, scouring the world of mages.

Ivar's entire tribe had been destroyed by the mages. Once upon a time he would have celebrated Raptus's victory. But he had learned since returning to Terra with Timothy that it was only a handful of powerful, cruel, and vindictive mages who were responsible for what had happened to the Asura. Like any other race, there was more good among them than bad.

The gyrocraft turned hard to the left, keeping well away from Raptus, swooping low over the heads of the mages. In the sky above them, farther to the north, Ivar could see the aerial battle. Verlis's clan fought fang and claw against Raptus's soldiers, tearing at one another, breathing fire. And on the rooftops, the acolytes of every guild had used up many of the magical weapons they'd been given and were now combating the Wurm with blades and axes and fundamental spells.

Death walked the streets of Arcanum that day, and it had already claimed far too many lives.

"Ivar, go!" Timothy shouted.

The Asura was ready. At the boy's word, he gripped the

metal bars of the gyro tightly and hurled himself out of the open back of the contraption. He spun in the air, twisting around so that after he'd fallen the ten feet to the broken, smoldering cobblestones, he landed in an easy crouch. Ivar glanced up to see Timothy veering back into the sky, flying the gyro away from Raptus just in case the monstrosity let loose another volley of fire.

"Caw! Caw!" cried Edgar, as the rook caught up to Ivar. He'd been following the gyro as quickly as he could. Now he circled around the Asura's head. "What are you waiting for? No time for standing around!"

Ivar nodded and turned, his gaze searching the grand-masters who stood now in the shadow of the giant Raptus. He spotted Cassandra and started running toward her.

"No time for much of anything," the rook said as he followed, his words nearly lost in the noisy chaos of the attack on Raptus.

Several mages shouted as they saw Ivar pass. He wondered if some of the older grandmasters were afraid he had betrayed them. But in the midst of the horror of this war, he couldn't have blamed them for finding fear in everything. Their deaths were but moments away.

Unless . . .

"Cassandra!" he shouted.

Edgar reached her first, cawing loudly and circling her head. Cassandra spun around, hands glowing with magic so white that it hurt Ivar's eyes to look at it. She saw him, and though she must have been in a frenzy, trapped in the panic of the moment, something in his face must have shaken her, for she whipped her hands up in a gesture that created a shield around all three of them, and she turned her back on Raptus . . . turned her back on death.

"Ivar, what is it? What's happened?"

"A message from Tim," he said grimly. "You must reach the Voice. A warning must be given to all of the mages still in Arcanum to evacuate the buildings, to get clear of every structure and into as open an area as possible."

Cassandra frowned. "What? I don't understand!"

Ivar reached for her hand. "You must."

Edgar paused in the air, wings beating, keeping him in place, a single black feather floating to the burned ground. "Remember when SkyHaven fell?"

If there had been horror on Cassandra's face before, now it was a picture of despair. She went white, mouth open, and the defensive shield she'd erected flickered with hesitation. But then her expression hardened and her eyes went cold.

Cassandra nodded. She had realized what Ivar already knew. There was no other way.

"With me!" she said, and she began to run.

Ivar and Edgar kept pace with her on the ground and in the air. All around them bits of ruin were burning. Grandmasters and combat mages were launching attacks up at Raptus. The air was charged with static. They ran past Arcturus Tot, who could not stand. It looked as though his legs were broken—perhaps when the wind of Raptus's wings had thrown him—but still he wielded powerful sorcery that formed a ball of greenish yellow energy between his hands . . . and then he hurled it at Raptus.

They did not slow to see what damage it might do.

Lord Romulus stood at the center of it all. He held a sword aloft and the blade seemed to be drawing lightning from the sky. No ordinary lightning; it was the indigo blue of the hour before dawn and the huge warrior's body shook with each touch of that power. Using magic, Romulus was tapping into the very nature of the world.

He lowered the sword, aiming its point at Raptus's chest. Lord Romulus shouted a battle cry as he rechanneled that magical energy at his enemy. The burst of destructive power that launched from the tip of his sword threw him backward, and he crashed to the ground with such force that his helmet cracked in two, one of the horns breaking off.

The attack was high. It struck Raptus in the snout. The monstrosity staggered backward two steps, left foot crushing the corpse of a dead combat mage. His snout was burned and gouged where the spell had struck him, and Raptus opened his maw to bellow in pain and rage.

He was wounded. But Lord Romulus had given everything that was within him, and Raptus still stood.

Dropping the remains of his helmet to the ground, Romulus stood and wearily raised his sword again.

But then Cassandra and Ivar were past him. Alethea Borgia stood with Lord Foxheart and several others, all of them working independently. This was what their defense had become, a scattering of powerful mages doing their best.

They had tried working their magic together and it had failed. Now they were just hoping an onslaught would do the job. Ivar knew they were just holding on to whatever hope remained.

The Voice held her staff in front of her and the magic that coalesced around its head was like churning liquid gold.

"Madame Voice!" Cassandra called.

Edgar came swooping down toward Alethea's head. Ivar wanted to shout to the bird to stop, that she might think she was under attack, but the Voice was neither rash nor foolish. The bird was lucky she had not batted him out of the air.

"Listen up!" the rook cried. "There's only one shot at this!"

"You have a plan?" the Voice demanded, staring at Cassandra and Ivar.

Even in the midst of this horror, Cassandra looked beautiful. Ivar could understand why Timothy liked her so much. But the girl was a grandmaster, and it was with all the weight of that duty that she turned now and looked at Ivar.

"No," she said. "But Timothy does."

Ivar nodded. "You must use the Voice to speak to every mage in Arcanum."

He told her again what Timothy had said about evacuation. And he told her why.

Edgar fluttered his wings and landed on Ivar's shoulder. "Most of the city's already empty. Only those who could fight stayed behind."

"But we've got to get the acolytes and tradecrafters out of those buildings right now!"

Alethea Borgia had been made the Voice of Parliament for good reason. Not only was she as powerful as nearly any other mage, but she had courage, cunning, and wisdom that had no rival. She saw immediately that there was no other choice.

Ivar felt humbled with respect for this woman.

The Voice clutched her staff. She turned to Foxheart and the others nearby. "Shield me!" she cried.

Cassandra went to aid them. As Ivar and Edgar watched, she helped Foxheart cast a spell that wove a powerful magical shield around the entire group. And the moment it was ready, the Voice held up her free hand, and golden light began to spray upward from her fingers and from the top of her staff, rushing into the air and spreading across the city like a shroud of glittering rain.

"Hear me, Arcanum!" she began, and Ivar felt her words resonating in his very bones, inside his skull, as though she spoke directly into his mind. *"I am the Voice of Parliament. You must hear me now, for your lives depend upon it."*

Edgar felt hope growing inside of him. He had been largely silent, trying his best to help where he could, distracting Wurm in the air for Timothy and Ivar. But what else could he do? He was just a rook, after all. Just a bird. Now he ruffled his wings, felt the heat of the aftereffects of Raptus's fire under his feathers, and he shifted on his perch on Ivar's shoulder.

He felt hopeful.

Then Ivar spoke. The Voice was not even finished with

her warning to the city, but the Asura cursed softly under his breath.

"What is it?" Edgar asked.

Ivar put a hand to his forehead. "We have forgotten, Edgar! What of Sheridan? He and the Wurm children . . . they won't hear the message. They'll still be inside the Cade house when it happens!"

Edgar was already flying. His tiny heart hammered in his chest and he beat his wings madly, slicing through the air with every bit of strength and speed that he could muster. Ivar's words were already lost on the wind behind him. Fear drove the rook on. No longer was he thinking about Raptus or the invading Wurm. There were shouts of furious mages reached him, and then there were screams. He felt heat behind him and a blast of searing air struck him. It meant that Raptus had let loose his volcanic fire again, that more mages and grandmasters had died, but to Edgar it was a blessing. It pushed him from behind, adding to his speed.

Frantic, the rook flew higher. Ahead was a beautiful building constructed by Phaestus, the most famous architectural mage in the history of Arcanum. It was beautiful, its outer shell a substance that caught all the colors of light and refracted them, making it a constantly shifting rainbow of soft hues. The top three floors were a massive bell tower, and it was from there that the loudest of the warning bells had sounded.

Now the bells were silent.

A battle was under way on the roof of that building.

Several of Raptus's raiders were harrying what appeared to be six or seven acolytes. Edgar saw two of the Wurm breathing fire that engulfed one of the mages, and the other acolytes attacked them with colorful bursts of destructive magic as well as swords. One acolyte wielded a huge ancient battle ax and leaped from the rooftop to land on the back of a Wurm.

There was blood.

Edgar tore his gaze away. He could not stop to help them. His destination was higher. Twenty feet above this battle, another was being waged. Verlis and Cythra were in mortal combat with a pair of Raptus's loyal soldiers.

Even as Edgar flew toward them, forcing himself to beat his wings even harder, a cold pit of dread grew inside him. He saw Cythra rip the wing off her enemy, sending the Wurm spiraling toward the ground. Then she helped Verlis to finish off the other.

They were about to fly down to the bell tower and help the acolytes when Edgar intercepted them. He flew right in front of Verlis's face.

"Cythra! Verlis! Stop!" he cried.

"Edgar?" Verlis snarled. "What are you doing?"

"Just listen!" the rook said, flapping madly to stay in place. "There's no way to defeat Raptus now that he's got the Spawn of Wrath in him. The only way to stop him is to take it away. Take the magic away. Timothy's going to try to get close enough, but if he can't . . . he's going to have to interrupt the matrix, like he did at SkyHaven fighting Alhazred.

And then all the magic will blink. We don't know for how long. Some of the buildings aren't made to stand without magic. They're all being evacuated. . . . The Voice is communicating with all the mages now—

"But Sheridan won't hear her. He's not a mage. Not even flesh and blood. He won't hear the warning!"

Cythra's eyes went wide. "No! The children!"

Verlis roared, fire pouring from his jaws, not in fury but in panic. Both of them turned toward August Hill and began to fly at speeds that Edgar could not hope to match. Still the rook pursued them. They raced across the sky above Arcanum, August Hill looming in the distance.

CHAPTER TWELVE

This isn't the way things are supposed to be, Timothy thought. He felt a terrible sadness and dread as he counted down the last seconds of the delay he had given himself, time for the Voice to warn the mages and for them to evacuate.

"Now," he muttered to himself.

Crossbow still gripped in his hands, he pressed the left foot pedal in the gyrocraft and it turned to the north, rotors humming. He had made his way around behind Raptus and now flew directly at the back of the gigantic Wurm's head. There were dangers in coming at Raptus from this direction. If he brought his wings up abruptly, he could knock Timothy out of the sky.

But that was better than being burned by his fire or swiped from the air by his talons. He didn't like the idea of a cowardly attack from behind, but Raptus was no ordinary enemy. Attacking him directly would be suicide. Sheer idiocy. There was no shame in avoiding that.

The air was superheated just from Raptus's presence, and it crackled with the magic that emanated from him. There were screams and shouts somewhere ahead, beyond the monster, but Timothy didn't allow himself to think about those or to wonder if his friends were still alive . . . if Cassandra was still alive.

He brought himself within thirty feet of the back of Raptus's head. The flesh was gnarled and tough like leather. His horns jutted upward, and for the first time Timothy noticed a smaller ridge of short, sharp horns that ran down the back of his skull.

"Now," he whispered again.

And he began. He took a deep breath and let it out slowly. There was so much magic in the air, both from Raptus and the mages combating him, that Timothy barely had to try in order to sense it all around him. But it wasn't just the surface—the magic went deep. There was the energy that ran everything, the spells that lifted sky carriages and kept doors locked, that held the souls of long-dead mages inside ghostfire lamps that lit cities and villages around the world . . . and then, much deeper, was the magical matrix, the reservoir of magic that all spells sprang from.

Timothy felt it all, the way he felt the wind on his face. If he had closed his eyes, he thought he would almost be able to see the layers of magic in the world.

The sorcerous power of Raptus was like a storm of

magic just in front of him. It displaced all the other magic around it.

With a mental push, Timothy forced his nullifying field out in front of him, stretching it outward, creating a zone in the air around him where there was no magic, where spells would not function. It was a bubble, expanding from the un-magician and his gyro, growing larger and larger. Raptus roared, and fire spilled over the sides of his huge jaws as he prepared for another flaming onslaught, ready to murder even more of the Parliament.

Timothy felt beads of sweat rolling down his forehead. He focused, imagining the nullifying field becoming an invisible sword, and then he reach out and touched Raptus . . . thrust that null field into him like a blade.

The connection was instant. It was as though Timothy were inside a tent, and the storm of magic whipped at the sides but could not touch him. Magic could never touch him, but oh, how it tried.

Raptus roared and arched his back, letting loose a stream of fire from his enormous maw, a volcanic explosion that sent liquid flame spouting into the air, the fire showering down across the ruin of buildings below. The Wurm—the dragon he had become—staggered forward a step, reaching around to try to touch the place where Timothy had cut into the magic that surged within him.

It was all Timothy could do to keep the gyro from spinning out of control and falling from the sky.

He could feel it even more then. The magic. The matrix.

In the air he could see phantoms flitting about, and he knew them for what they were, had seen them before. Now he was tapping so deeply into the matrix that somehow, he could see them again. They were the souls of mages long dead, men and women whose spirits, whose magic, helped power the matrix and the world. Timothy had planned to just attack Raptus. To touch him the way he had done Nicodemus once upon a time, to just turn off his magic for a moment.

It wasn't working. There was too much raw magical power in Raptus. A touch would disrupt it, but to shut it down would require more than that.

Timothy gritted his teeth. Raptus staggered again and turned, searching for the source of this attack. The wind whipped the gyro, and Timothy worked his foot pedals to keep it straight.

Raptus spotted him.

The boy forced his terror away, raised his crossbow and fired. The shaft flew straight and true and struck the dragon in the eye. Raptus roared, half blinded, and in that moment the magic inside him, the power, wavered.

Timothy shouted with the effort as he spread his nullifying field out farther, and the bubble grew large enough that it engulfed Raptus. All along, Timothy had suspected that the Spawn of Wrath, the enchantment that had turned Raptus into this towering monstrosity, was drawing from the well of power, the depths of the magical matrix itself. Now he knew it to be true. He felt it.

He had wanted to avoid this at any cost, but now he knew he had no choice. Raptus had slaughtered half the Parliament already, and if Timothy did not stop him, he would destroy Arcanum, and then the world.

He had to cut Raptus off from the matrix, so the Spawn of Wrath could not leech any more power from it. To undo that spell, the ancient magic of the Dragons of Old, he had to disrupt the matrix itself.

Just for a moment.

Once before the un-magician had touched the matrix, pushed his nullifying field into the very fabric of power that pulsed through the world. Now he did it again.

Timothy could feel all the magic around him, and with a shout of sadness and fear and effort, he *pushed* his nullifying field with all of his might.

He felt the matrix give way.

The magic winked out.

From far below he heard all the mages who still lived cry out in surprise and alarm.

Raptus roared in pain and spread his wings, but he seemed to be falling. It took Timothy only a moment to realize that his eyes were deceiving him. Raptus was not falling at all.

He was shrinking.

The Spawn of Wrath had been undone, the spell destroyed. The Wurm's power had been taken away. In seconds he collapsed in size, diminishing with astonishing speed. Raptus roared with pain as his bones and flesh reknitted themselves, but his voice was smaller now and no longer shook the sky.

The last time Timothy had done this, disrupted the matrix, it had lasted two or three seconds.

There were screams now and shouts of panic and a distant rumble like thunder. Timothy looked around, and it took him a moment to understand what had happened. What he had done.

The matrix had not blinked out this time. It had not shuddered.

It had shut down.

The magic was gone.

Not far away a massive building—home to some guild or other and constructed so delicately that magic held it up—began to fall.

Edgar was flying after Verlis and Cythra, wings beating so hard that they seemed on fire with exertion. The moment he had warned the Wurm couple what Timothy was going to attempt—and what the consequences might be—they had taken off across the sky. Their children were at the Cade estate, after all. And not only their children, but all the children of their clan. The warning had gone out, the Voice had used magic to speak to all the mages in Arcanum, but Sheridan was nothing more than a man of metal and would not have heard such a warning.

August Hill loomed ahead. Verlis and Cythra were two dark slashes in the morning sky ahead, but Edgar did his best to keep up. He flew onward, wings growing more tired as he went higher and higher, rising toward the peak of August Hill. Far ahead and above, he saw the two panicked Wurm, Cythra and Verlis, reach the Cade estate. They circled once around the top of the massive old house.

From behind—back the way he had come—Edgar heard a thunderous roar that became a scream of fury. Raptus's fury. But there was panic in the sound as well.

The rook could not wield magic—but it was in him. He felt it. So when the very air itself rippled as though a wave of magic had swept over him, he dipped a wing and turned just for a moment, glancing back to see what had happened.

He heard a rumble like a massive ground quake and saw, back near the place where the remaining members of Parliament had been fighting Raptus, a tall, cone-shaped building begin to fall apart. To crumble. The top tipped to one side and collapsed.

Far, far in the distance, where the city gave way to the eastern coast, he could see the shape of SkyHaven hanging magically above the ocean. He was high enough, and his eyes keen enough, to make out the shape of its battlements and towers, and the jagged underside of rock and earth that made up the foundation of that floating fortress.

Even as he caught sight of it, he realized it was falling. To Edgar it was like a nighmare. It seemed so strange that he could see SkyHaven tumble from the air, but not hear it, that the angle of his view and the buildings out near the edge of the city blocked his sight just enough that he knew it had fallen into the ocean, but did not see it splash down and begin to sink.

The fortress had been evacuated. He hoped no one had been foolish enough to stay behind. That no one had—

"No!" he screeched, spinning around and darting again toward August Hill.

He caught just a glimpse of Cythra entering from one of those upper-story balconies. Verlis must already have gone inside. Edgar cawed loudly and tried to cry out to them, but he knew he was much too far away to be heard. He flew with all his strength, ignoring the pain in his muscles. His eyes were wide with terror, and when he began to hear more shouts and more rumbling in the city behind him— other buildings supported by magic crashing down—he did not bother to turn.

All the magic in Arcanum had gone away. Timothy had somehow cut the world off from the matrix, or even—as terrifying a thought as it was—shut the matrix itself down. *The grand observatory would crumble,* Edgar thought. The aviary where he had been born would also tear itself apart, its architecture not made to stand without magic. The tower of the Spiral Guild would never hold together. So many.

So many.

"Verlis!" Edgar shouted.

Now the Cade estate loomed ahead. Edgar flew, a couple of black feathers tearing loose and floating down toward the mountainside below. August Hill rose up in front of him. The home that Argus Cade had built was a grand old thing, dangling there on the cliffside.

"Cythra! Verlis! Get them out now!" Edgar screamed.

He felt as though he would drop from the sky himself in exhaustion. Edgar did not bother to go toward the front door, but flew above it. The rook pinned his wings back and soared like a bullet toward the same open balcony door that the Wurm had used.

Below him, the stone stairs in front of the Cade estate cracked off and dropped into space, striking the mountain-side far below and shattering into rubble.

Edgar cried out in horror and veered off, turning quickly around to watch for any Wurm—parents or children—to emerge. He scanned the windows for some sign of Sheridan, his friend. His best friend.

Then the Cade estate collapsed under its own weight. The corner where it was attached to August Hill remained anchored and so it fell at an angle, the whole house tilting down. Walls shattered and buckled, and then it was tearing itself apart. The entire structure that had served as the home of Argus Cade, and which Timothy had inherited, rolled down August Hill and became nothing but rubble.

The rook screamed.

Timothy landed the gyrocraft in the vast area where the battle had taken place, where all the buildings had already been destroyed and there was no chance of him being crushed by crumbling architecture. The worst part was, he felt that perhaps he ought to be crushed. He had stopped Raptus, true enough, but at what cost? The magic had rippled and then winked out, and he had been waiting with every passing second for it to blink back on again, just as it had done when he had defeated Alhazred. Now, he did not know what was going to happen.

All he knew was that dozens of buildings around the city were falling down, and it was his fault. Most of them, perhaps even all, had been entirely empty. The city had been evacuated except for those who remained behind to fight. He supposed some of the acolytes might have been killed in the aftermath of the magical power outage. But he didn't want to think about it right now.

The gyro landed roughly, something cracking as he set it down. Timothy didn't care. He flung the crossbow aside and climbed out. As he did, he scanned the square where only a minute before, Raptus had been preparing to burn the rest of Parliament to death. Some of the mages were in a circle far away from him, and he suspected he knew what they were doing. Surrounding Raptus. Capturing him, perhaps even killing him.

He looked to the northward sky and saw that there were only a handful of enemy Wurm still there, fighting members of Verlis's clan.

The battle was all but over.

"Timothy!"

He heard the voice, knew who it belonged to, but still he was reluctant to face her. His own power had caused just as much disaster as Raptus's dream of conquest and vengeance.

"Tim!" she called again.

He turned to face Cassandra. She ran toward him, her smile relieved and exuberant. Timothy could not help it. Despite the weight of guilt on him, he smiled in return. To see her looking at him like that, her green eyes lit with pleasure at the sight of him . . . all he could do was open his arms and embrace her when she came to him.

Cassandra held him tight and whispered his name several times. Timothy kissed her hair, and then she pulled away, reached up to cup his jaw in her palm, and guided his face to hers. Their lips met and the kiss was like a balm to soothe the pain in his heart.

"I . .. . caused this," he said as she pulled away. He searched her eyes. "All of these buildings . . . the magic . . ."

She shuddered, and pain rippled across her features. Cassandra nodded. "I know. It's . . . being without it, that's going to take some getting used to. But it's only temporary, right? The magic being gone. It'll come back any minute, I'm sure."

Timothy shrugged. He made sure she saw his eyes when he said, "I don't know."

Her face paled as that worry settled in. Cassandra was as shocked as he knew all the other mages would be. But then she knitted her brows, seeing his own worry and pain. She reached up to touch his cheek, this time making sure that he would look into her eyes.

"You did what you had to do to stop Raptus. Whatever the sacrifice . . . it can't be as terrible as the massacre of an entire city, as the enslavement of all the mages of the world."

Timothy understood her point, but it didn't make him feel any better.

Across the ruined square he saw some of the mages turning away from where they had taken Raptus prisoner, the mighty Wurm so drained now that he was no match for so many mages, even without their magic. Small gouts of fire flew into the air, the diminished Wurm, the defeated tyrant, trying until the end to have his revenge. Among those mages, Timothy saw the Voice, Alethea Borgia, pull Lord Romulus aside. She pointed across the smoldering rubble at Timothy and Cassandra. Several of the others looked their way as well, including Foxheart and Tarquine.

All of them without magic now. For the moment they could not be grandmasters, because without magic there could be no guilds for them to lead. They were just people. Warriors and politicians. Just people.

They began to walk across the square toward Timothy, and he steeled himself to tell them the truth. He didn't know how to turn the magic back on. He didn't know how long it would be gone, or if the matrix had been damaged forever.

The air rippled beside Timothy. He felt Ivar's presence a moment before the Asura made himself visible, letting the pigment return to his skin. One moment it was as though Cassandra and Timothy were alone, and then Ivar was simply there.

His eyes were full of grief.

"Timothy—"

"Ivar!" the boy said. "You're okay! Thank the moons you're okay!"

But only then did he see the grimness of his friend's expression.

"What is it?" he asked.

"Ivar?" Cassandra said. "What's happened?"

The Asura glanced away a moment, off toward August Hill, then back to Timothy. "Your father's house . . . your house . . . when the warning went out, Sheridan could not have heard. Verlis and Cythra and Edgar went to carry the warning themselves, but—"

"No," Timothy said, a fist of grief clutching his heart. "Oh, no."

The boy glanced upward, saw several Wurm flying toward the ruined square now that their enemies had been captured or destroyed. Timothy began waving to them frantically.

"Here! Down here! Hello, is that Torga? And Usbek! Come down, come down! Hurry!"

They spiraled down to alight on the ruined cobblestones beside him. Timothy ranted, racing through an explanation of his plan and his fears of what might happen. Their eyes lit up with terror. Torga's own children were among those at the house. She picked him up in her arms as though she were embracing him after a long time apart. Usbek picked up Cassandra.

"You have to explain to the others," Timothy told the Asura as the Wurm hoisted him and Cassandra off the ground and they began to fly toward August Hill. Tim could see Romulus and the Voice hurrying toward the place where Ivar now stood alone. Romulus shouted something at Timothy, but the boy did not hear a word of it. The wind stole it away.

For two hours he and Cassandra led the search for survivors from the collapse of the Cade estate. The remains of the house were strewn up and down August Hill. The search would have gone much more quickly with magic, but of course no one had any left. With every passing moment the shroud of despair and panic grew in the city. Mages were wondering what to do now that they had no magic. Most of them did not even know how to bathe without the help of spellcasting.

But some of the mages—and all of the surviving Wurm from Verlis's clan—put aside such fears and questions for another time. They worked feverishly, sorting through the rubble strewn up and down August Hill, to no avail.

Eventually Cassandra forced Timothy to take a rest.

Edgar, who had been sifting through rubble himself, as best he could, settled down on a shattered wooden beam beside him.

"If only I'd been faster," the rook said, ruffling his feathers.

Timothy shook his head. "You'd only have been in the building when it fell. You'd have . . . gone, with them."

Edgar cocked his head at a strange angle. "Maybe I should have. Better that than know I couldn't do anything."

A long shadow fell across Timothy. It was Lord Romulus.

Without his ruined helmet he was still imposing, but on this day his face was etched with grief and kindness. He was a man of good heart.

"Anything?" Timothy asked the man.

Romulus frowned, deeply troubled. "Not a thing. No survivors, but no bodies, either. We haven't found a wing or a claw. We know they were all in there, the Wurm children as well as Verlis and Cythra. But it's like the house was empty when it all fell apart."

Timothy grimaced and stared at the sky. It was clear and perfect, the kind of sky that always made him think of home. Not here, not the home of his birth and now his home by choice, but home back on the Island of Patience . . .

A small smile lifted the corners of his mouth. He glanced at Romulus. "No trace at all. Nothing. Like they weren't even there?"

Lord Romulus nodded.

Timothy sprang to his feet, laughed, and clapped his hands once. "Good old Sheridan!" he cried, understanding at last what had happened, realizing that Verlis and Cythra had gotten their warning to the house in time after all. "Good old Sheridan."

He shook his head, grinning.

"Well done."

EPILOGUE

The Xerxis still stood.

Half a day had passed since the defeat of Raptus and the devastation of so much of Arcanum. The people who had been evacuated from the city had been told it might be many days before they were allowed to return. Without magic, every building had to be inspected to see if its construction was solid enough to stand on its own. No one could return to those structures until they were proven safe.

The combat mages and acolytes and Wurm who had survived were working together now to clear some of the rubble and tend to the dead. Most of Raptus's soldiers had been killed or captured, but some had been driven off. Raptus himself was reportedly still unconscious, but being held under Wurm guard in a jail cell in the Arcanum head-quarters of the Legion Nocturne. He would not escape.

Timothy had been asked by Cassandra to come with her to the Xerxis, where the surviving members of Parliament were to gather to discuss the future of Arcanum. Messengers were being dispatched to ride on horseback out to other cities and villages. No other communication was available. Timothy had wanted nothing more than to go with her, but he could not even consider entering the Xerxis now, or appearing before Parliament.

Not after what he'd done.

Instead he sat in a small room at the University of Saint Germain. At Cassandra's request, her new assistant had arranged with the headmaster for Timothy and his friends to stay there until other accommodations could be found. With both his father's house and SkyHaven destroyed, he had nowhere else to go. For the past hour he had done nothing but lie on the rough mattress in the dormitory room. Edgar was perched on the windowsill, peering out at the city. From time to time he would fly out the open window and survey the damage, then return to report any news.

Ivar sat perfectly still on the floor near the door, a sentinel, watching over Timothy. The Asura did not have to say it, but Timothy was aware that Ivar was protecting him. There would undoubtedly be mages who hated him for what he had done, no matter what his reasoning. It was as though he had stripped each of them of their arms or legs. Magic was as much a part of them as those limbs, and Timothy had crippled them.

The thought made him cringe. He thought of Sheridan,

and of Verlis and Cythra and the Wurm children, all of whom were trapped on the Island of Patience, in a parallel dimension that could not be reached without magic. They were stuck there unless and until the matrix could be restored. He thought of those mages who were his friends— particularly Caiaphas and, remarkably, Lord Romulus—and the knowledge of what he had done to them made him shudder and draw himself into a tight ball on the bed. Caiaphas had been badly injured during the war for Arcanum. He would recover completely, but there would be scars.

Timothy knew he was to blame, and he let himself burn with guilt for a time.

And then he frowned, and scowled in disgust at his reaction.

He sat up.

Ivar raised an eyebrow and studied him.

"Tim. Are you all right?" Edgar asked, fluttering his wings. The blackbird cocked his head, obviously concerned.

"No," the boy admitted. "But I can't hide forever."

"You have no reason to hide," Ivar told him. "You saved them. All of them. Perhaps you even saved the world."

Timothy sighed, nodding. "Maybe. But you saw the way they looked at me. You heard the things some of them said. There are mages out there who would rather be dead than have all their magic taken away."

"Hey," Edgar said, "it might come back."

"Probably. It will probably come back," Timothy agreed.

"But there are no guarantees. That's not much comfort to them. It's as though I've taken their hearts."

"They live," Ivar said firmly. "Their families live, because of you. The collapse of the matrix is a crisis, yes, but magic is not life."

Timothy had nothing to say to that. He was sure that most of the mages would not see it quite so simply.

In the silence of that moment, there came a knock at the door. Ivar sprang to his feet and set himself in a defensive posture as he opened it. Timothy saw him visibly relax and was relieved when Ivar stepped aside to let Cassandra into the room.

He loved her. But he did not go to her right away. After what he had done, he wasn't sure how she would feel.

"Hello," he said.

"Hello," she replied, and he saw a glint of hurt in her eyes and knew he had been wrong to be so distant.

"I'm sorry," he said. "I just don't know how to speak to anyone right now. I can't imagine what they're saying about me."

Cassandra smiled softly and shook her head. She went to him and took his hands in hers. "They're saying that you did what you had to do. They're saying that without you, all would have been lost."

She tucked a lock of red hair behind her ear and offered a small shrug. "Or, at least, that's what most of them are saying. And no one is listening to the others. We were all out there, Tim. We all felt the panic of knowing that we had lost, that we were dead. Raptus had won. Even those who are wishing some other solution could have been found cannot deny the fire and blood that they saw with their own eyes. And besides, the Voice and Lord Romulus are proclaiming you a champion of Arcanum. No one is going to argue with them today."

Timothy blinked and stared at her. "A . . . champion?"

Cassandra reached up to touch his face. "Of course! If you'd only seen yourself, you'd understand."

"You were pretty impressive, kid," Edgar said from the windowsill, ruffling his feathers. "I'm proud of you."

"As am I," Ivar agreed.

Timothy shook his head, hardly able to believe it. "But the magic—"

"Will be back," Cassandra said. "We all agree on that. Energy cannot be destroyed, Tim. It is still there, somewhere. Eventually we will find a way to tap into it again. We are mages, after all. But until we do, Lord Romulus has reminded the Parliament that there is only one person in all the world who truly knows how to survive without the aid of magic."

Ivar smiled, even laughed a bit, though softly, and crossed his arms as he gazed expectantly at Timothy.

"You mean . . . ?" he began.

Cassandra nodded. "Of course. They need you now more than ever. There's no more ghostfire, though. We've put the souls of all of our ancestors to rest at last. But someone must teach them how to harness the hungry fire, and show them how to run water for bathing and to irrigate crops. There are so many things that we relied upon magic for. They need you, Tim. We need you."

She gazed up at him with those green eyes that took his breath away, and then Cassandra slid her arms around him.

"*I* need you."

Timothy smiled.

Perhaps there was hope for the future after all.

On the Island of Patience, Sheridan sat on an outcropping of rock that jutted into the ocean. It had been one of Timothy's favorite places on the island. Sheridan and Ivar had often referred to it as his "peaceful spot." Timothy had liked to simply sit there and watch the waves or lay back and observe the clouds drifting across the sky.

Now Sheridan sat with his metal hands on his knees and gazed at the sky, watching the Wurm children laughing and shouting as they chased one another, darting and weaving through the air. Blasts of fire burned across the sky as they attacked one another, but it was all in play. None of them would actually get burned, as long as they did not get out of hand. And Sheridan was there to see that they did not.

One of the children, a young male Wurm named Trajun, had flown too high, and several of the others were pursuing him, their wings outstretched.

Sheridan stood, a loud whistle of steam coming from the valve on the side of his head.

"Trajun! Lystra! All of you, come back down!" he called. "You know you aren't supposed to stray far from the island!"

Several of them glared at him, but they obeyed. Sheridan did not want them to be sad. He hated having to curtail their exuberance, but Verlis and Cythra had made sure that all the children knew the rules. They were going to have to survive here until Timothy and Cassandra figured out a way to reach them, to come through and bring them back to Terra. The children had learned to speak in the tongue of mages from Sheridan. They might bristle at times, but they usually obeyed him. And the adults had made it clear to them that Sheridan was in charge.

Verlis and Cythra had gone searching across the ocean for other islands, or any land that would provide more food than Patience had to offer. It was a small island. There were enough fruits and vegetables for them to survive in the short term, but Cythra did not want the children to ever be hungry. So she and Verlis hoped to find additional resources elsewhere.

Sheridan was not so concerned. As lonely as it would be without Timothy, he would enjoy being back on the island. After all, Patience was his home. And he knew Timothy would find a way to get to him eventually. It might take years, but Sheridan could wait.

He had faith.